Falling Inn Love

ERIN BRANSCOM

Falling Inn Love

Freedom Valley Series

Copyright © 2022 by Erin Branscom

ALL RIGHTS RESERVED. This book contains material protected under International and Federal Copyright Laws and Treaties. Any unauthorized reprint or use of this material is prohibited. No part of this book may be reproduced or transmitted in any form or by any means, electronic or mechanical, including photocopying, recording, or by an information and retrieval system without express written permission from the Author/Publisher.

This is a work of fiction. Names, characters, places, and incidents either are the product of the author's imagination or are used fictitiously, and any resemblance to actual persons, living or dead, business establishments, events, or locales is entirely coincidental.

Made in the United States of America.

ISBN: 979-8-88662-000-9 (ebook)
ISBN: 979-8-88662-001-6 (paperback)

Editor: Francine LaSala
Copy Editor: Brooke Crites
Proofreading: Brooke Crites
Formatting: Enni from Yummy Book Covers
Cover Design: Enni from Yummy Book Covers

For Francine. None of this would be possible without your support, encouragement, and unwavering belief in me. I will be forever grateful for you. You are the catalyst for everything in my writing career that follows. This one is for you. I hope all of you reading this find a Francine in your life. Someone who believes in you and encourages you even when your dream is just beginning and not at its best yet.

Sensitive Content Warning

This book contains some heavy-hearted content. My little brother Michael was killed in October of 2020 while driving to work in the morning when he was hit by a nurse who was driving herself to work while impaired. She destroyed so many lives that day. This book is dedicated to anyone who has been devastated by the horrific effects of impaired drivers. I hope that this book can bring hope and healing to anyone who has lost a loved one and provide awareness. I wrote this book because sometimes we can feel so alone in our pain when terrible things have happened to us. You're not alone.

We're in this world together.

Love, Erin

CHAPTER 1

Beth

No. There's no one.

I wasn't sure where I'd end up today, but this sure as hell wasn't it.

"Great. Just freaking great," I mutter as steam pours out from under the hood of my ten-year-old green Subaru. My car smells awful, like something burning or melting.

I pull off to the side of the road and park, a sitting duck in my no-longer-trustworthy SUV, hoping I'm not going to be turned into roadkill by a big semi coming down the highway.

I reach across the seat and pull my phone over to me by the charging cord. Thankfully, it's fully charged.

"Where the hell am I?" I cringe as I open a navigation app. Freedom Valley, New Hampshire.

I cup my face with my hands. My chest tightens as I begin to cry. I'm running out of money and time, and it's starting to get dark out. Hot tears streak my cheeks. I just want to go home, but I don't have a home anymore; I haven't for the past six years. Nowadays, home is this nomadic lifestyle I've chosen for myself.

I hear a light tapping on the window and look up to see a tall, dark-haired man with the most gorgeous light green eyes peering down at me.

Great. Now this is the part where I get murdered on a highway all alone.

I roll the window down a little and the man leans in, looking concerned. "Are you okay?"

"Yeah, I'll be fine. I just pulled over for a rest," I say, forcing a smile and wiping my eyes, quickly trying to look away and not stare too long. His hair topples over his forehead as he inches closer. He has a full, dark beard that makes me weak in the knees.

Are beards out? Because if they are, they should definitely be back in. This guy makes it work. I've never seen a more gorgeous man, and this beard makes him dark, scary, and handsome all at the same time.

"Are you sure? I think something is wrong with your car. If I had to guess, I'd say it's the radiator. Do you want me to take a look?" He cringes as he turns his head away from the awful, acrid smell of the smoke continuing to barrel out of the hood.

It occurs to me that I could possibly be his next intended victim on this lonely New Hampshire two-lane highway, where no one would ever hear me scream. He doesn't look like a murderer, but I'm basically an expert in *Dateline* and forensics and murder shows on Netflix, so here we are. Where it all probably ends.

He holds up his hands and says with a smile, "I'm Evan."

"Hi," I say quietly.

"Hi," he replies softly, his eyes taking in my face with curiosity. "Can I help you? I can't just leave you here. My mom would kill me."

Great. A family of murderers. Hey, I've seen that movie Wrong Turn.

"Okay, but can I stay in the car?" I ask. I'm nervous. I am all alone out here and I don't know this guy.

"Yep, just pop the hood," he says, then walks to his old retro truck parked in front of me with its hazards blinking.

I take him in. He's even nice-looking from the back, as well. Maybe even more so. Why am I admiring this stranger's backside? This isn't good.

He's tall, wearing form-fitting jeans and brown boots. He's not wearing the flannel. It's wearing him. *Damn. He's a walking lumberjack snack.* He pulls a pair of gloves from his truck and strolls back to my car, using his gloves to lift the hot hood that seems to have finally stopped steaming.

From the safety of my car, I hear him messing around with some things before he shuts the hood and taps on my window. I roll it down again, still unsure of this guy.

"It's your radiator, so I wouldn't drive it anymore. It needs to be towed into town to Sam's to get looked at. I can give you a ride to wherever you're going," he says as he tucks his gloves into his back pocket.

I nod, my chest tightening up again. "Okay, but I don't know where to go. I was staying in my car and dry camping," I admit, looking out the window. I realize I shouldn't have told him I have nowhere to go, but what other options do I have?

A car zips past us, making me jump. When I glance back at him, I notice he's still staring at me, looking a little bit in shock.

"Staying in your car? Is that safe?" he asks, his eyes narrowing like he wants to give me a dad lecture.

"I have nowhere to go or stay now," I say motioning to my car. "This was my plan."

He strokes his chin, looking frustrated. "Grab whatever you need for tonight and I'll take you to the inn up the road. I know the owner. You can stay there until you figure out your car."

"Why would you do that?" I ask nervously, crossing my

arms, starting to shiver.

"Because if my mom and sister knew that I left you out here on the side of the road and didn't help you, they'd be really angry. And trust me, you do not want to see those two angry or disappointed. It's the worst. Come on, get your stuff, we don't have all night. I'll give you a lift and call the tow for you. It'll be fine."

I finally just blurt it out. "Are you a murderer? How do I know you won't kill me and bury me in the woods somewhere out here?"

He sizes me for a minute then bursts out laughing. "You're funny. Come on, get your things. You'll be fine. I only murder on the weekends."

"It's Friday. It *is* the weekend."

"Fine, I only murder on holidays," he deadpans with a smile, rolling his eyes and turning to look down the road.

"If you murder me, I will come back as a ghost and haunt you for the rest of your life."

"Fair enough," he says as he shrugs his shoulders, looking like he's trying to hide another smile.

I take a deep breath and gather up my phone, charger, and purse.

"Is that all you'll need for a few nights? It might be a few days before Sam can fix this."

I get out and open the trunk, pulling out my overnight bag. Before I can sling it over my shoulder, Evan gently takes it from me and steps back.

"Anything else?" he asks.

I lift my laptop backpack out of the car, then lock up and walk toward Evan's truck. He tucks my bag into the back and opens the passenger door for me. He has this nice, warm, small-town vibe, and it works for him. I still hope he's not a murderer, though, because what a waste of a good-looking guy that would be.

"I like your truck," I say, glancing around at it. It has an old, worn but colorful blanket on the bench, probably to conceal decades of wear and tear.

"Thanks. It was my grandfather's and then my father's. It makes me feel close to them when I drive it."

Wow, that is heartwarming. I couldn't imagine having anything of my mothers, let alone my grandmother's.

"Where are you coming from?" he asks as he pulls back onto the road.

I debate over how much is too much to tell him, but I've already jumped in his truck with him, so what's the point of holding back now? He seems like a nice guy, and he's definitely attractive. I watch his profile as he drives, his green eyes striking against his dark beard and his big hands... *Okay, focus, Beth. Geez.*

"Boston," I say, glancing out the window as the scenery changes to beautiful fall foliage along the road to the inn.

He's playing eighties music—which I love—on the radio.

He turns it down to ask, "So, what brings you to Freedom Valley?"

"I'm a writer and I travel around for work. I was looking for a place to stay for a few weeks to finish a project and see New England in the fall. What about you? What do you do?"

"You're looking for work?" he replies, ignoring my question.

He's misunderstood what I do for a living, but to be honest, the writing has not been going well lately. I've been doing various admin jobs and some bartending between writing projects, and I could use the extra cash again now, so I nod.

"I think the inn might be looking to hire a front desk manager. Would you be interested if it's still available?"

"Yes."

He turns onto a winding road that leads up to a big white inn with a beautiful white sign that reads *The Golden Gable Inn* in gold script. There's a large main building with a lot of small cottages around it. Hunter green shutters grace the front, making it feel more like a home than a hotel. The large front porch stretches across the front of the main house and has white rocking chairs and potted mums of various fall colors bunched around the chairs and pumpkins stacked on both sides of the doors. It is one of the most comforting places I've ever seen. It feels like coming home. To a real home. I thought places like this only existed in Hallmark movies.

My heart pulls as I remember my small front porch in Texas that I decorated similarly with a fall wreath, pumpkins, and mums every year. Autumn has always been my favorite season and my heart feels sad to think I no longer have a home to decorate.

I start to panic because there's no way I can afford to stay here for a night, let alone a few nights, and I definitely don't want to owe this guy any favors. I'm still not sure why he's helping me. I want to trust people, but history has taught me not to trust anyone, including random strangers who are eager to help. There's a good reason I keep to myself and don't talk to very many people while traveling. I've come across a few creeps.

"Evan, I don't think I can afford this. I'm sorr—"

"Relax. I know the owners. I'm sure they'll be more than happy to set you up for a few days." He smiles at me reassuringly.

Evan parks and grabs my bag from the back. As we walk up the steps, I run my hand over the railing and glance around at the fall leaves, breathing in the autumn air. It's getting dark and I'm relieved to not be stuck on the highway anymore.

"It's a pretty special place," he says as we walk through the entrance. "Been in the same family for three generations now. You'll love it here."

We head up to the desk and I set my backpack down. I

freeze when Evan walks behind the desk and begins typing on the keyboard.

"What are you doing?" I ask, confused.

He smiles sheepishly at me. "Told you I knew the owner."

"Evan, honey, is that you?" a voice calls from the back as a short, round woman with a cropped, white-blonde bob and bright green eyes approaches.

She kisses Evan on the cheek before turning to me and smiling warmly. "Who do we have here? Checking in? I'm Margie, welcome to The Golden Gable Inn."

I turn to Evan, unsure what to say. It dawns on me that she might be his mother. Their eyes match, but other than that, they don't look alike.

Finally, I say, "Hi, I'm Beth Markwell. I'm not sure what I'm doing just yet…"

Evan, still typing, says, "She'll be checking in for the weekend."

"You work here?" I ask in disbelief, looking at him while this woman curiously watches me.

"Yes, my family owns the inn," he says. "Okay, I've got a queen bed available on the first floor. Will that work?" he asks, his green eyes peering at me, his gaze lingering on my mouth as he bites his bottom lip.

Holy shit. This man melts me like butter in a pan just from looking at him. I know I just met him, but I feel this connection with him. I don't think I've ever felt instant electricity with someone like this, but I can feel it radiating off him, too. It isn't just me.

"I don't know how I can pay you," I reply nervously. I wish the world would swallow me up, I'm so embarrassed.

The woman tilts her head and asks, "Where are you from, honey?"

Okay, I'm from the south where people are typically overly friendly—you know, the whole southern hospitality thing. But so far, everyone is even nicer here. I'm hesitant to talk about myself, but something feels different here. I slowly feel my guard letting down, and if I'm being honest, it actually feels good.

"Originally Austin, Texas. I travel a lot now; I'm a writer. I was hoping to stay in the area for a while, if I can find a place to stay and find part-time work."

She looks at Evan and murmurs, "No show on our interview today." Then she turns to me. "Well, we could use some help around here for a while. Would you be available to lend a hand? Front desk help, maybe in the dining room, too, if we need it?"

I hesitate for a moment then realize I have no other options. "Sure," I finally say. Thankfully, the murderer vibes aren't here.

Evan slides a key on a vintage-white, worn motel keychain with the inn's logo in gold script and a form across the desk for me to sign.

I sign it and slide it back, palming the key. Evan then picks up my bag and heads down the hall.

"I'm glad I found you and that you're safe," he says as I catch up to him. "I can't imagine my sister breaking down like that and not having anywhere safe to go. Is there anyone you can call?" he asks.

My shoulders sag. I miss having a person to call.

"No, there's no one," I say quietly.

CHAPTER 2

Evan

I'm in over my head.

My heart breaks in two with the way her lip trembles and her eyes fill with tears when she says she has no one to call. I want to scoop her up and hug her right there, but I'm not typically one to go around hugging strangers, even beautiful strangers. Plus, given that she's already concerned I may be a murderer, I can't imagine touching her is a great call right now.

"Okay, it's no problem," I say softly. "I'm going to give Sam a call. He runs the auto shop here in Freedom Valley and he's the best. It'll all work out, okay?"

Her eyes meet mine briefly and, in a skeptical tone, she

asks, "You really run this inn?"

"Do I not look like an innkeeper?" I reply, crossing my arms and leaning back against the wall. It's been a while since I've been around a woman that intrigues me. She's beautiful, and her puzzled expression makes me want to tease her about the inn.

"Not really what I would have guessed," she says.

"You and me both," I mutter as I watch a few guests make their way to check-in.

She tips her head back down for a moment, and says, "Thank you for all your help. I mean it. I don't know what I would have done if I was stranded on the side of the road tonight, I really appreciate your help. When do you want me to start?"

She finally lifts her head. The old cap she's wearing has been pulled low, but I can still see her beautiful eyes. They're a cross between blue and green. She has no makeup on but her face is glowing. Her long, blond hair is pulled through the back of her cap. She's wearing jeans, a black vintage Fleetwood Mac *Rumors* t-shirt, and white Converse. She's curvy and petite and seems authentic and interesting. Like someone I want to get to know more. There's something about her I just can't put my finger on... Something sad and beautiful at the same time. I want to know what happened to her.

She pauses in the doorway, I guess waiting for my

response. I shake myself from staring at her. "Breakfast is from seven to ten in the dining room. Just come find me then and we'll work it out."

A comfortable warmth fills her face and she meets my eyes. "Thanks, Evan." She grabs her bag and heads inside, shutting the door.

I'm in trouble with this one, I think to myself as I head back to the front desk.

My mom has already checked in the new guests by the time I return. She smiles at me. "Picked up another stray?"

"Well, the last one I brought back ended up being the best employee we've ever had," I say smugly, raising an eyebrow.

"Ah-hem." Sasha, our chef, appears just then and glares at me. "Best employee?" she teases, playful disdain in her tone.

"Second best," I assure her. "You know you're my number one."

Sasha is married to our handyman, Pete. They've been with the inn for over fifteen years now and have become like older siblings to me.

She rolls her eyes, indicating the conversation is over, and hands me a sheet of paper.

"I changed the menu a bit for next week," she explains. "Nothing big. Just using up some things we have. Trying to save money on our grocery orders."

I realize what she's doing and I'm grateful, although I feel a stab of guilt in my gut. Sasha knows we're having trouble and she's trying to save us money. I haven't told my mom much about our financial issues because I don't want to worry her when we already have enough going on. I quickly try to change the subject.

I glance through her suggestions quickly. "Looks good, Sasha. We have a guest who's going to be helping up front for a few days. Her name is Beth."

"And how long will we be keeping this one? Mellie is going on months. Not that I'm complaining." She straightens her apron then heads back to the kitchen.

She's definitely not complaining. Mellie is the hardest-working employee we have. She keeps this place in tip-top shape and we'd never be able to find another housekeeper like her. And her four-year-old son Kase is an added bonus. I love that kid, we all do.

Mellie showed up with Kase several months back, in need of work and a place for them to stay. She's also become family to us.

I don't find the staff, they find us, and it magically works out. I turn to my mom. "See? I've got this innkeeping thing down. It's not much different than being a Marine."

My mom ignores my teasing and tilts her head, eyebrows drawing together. "Have you heard from your sister today?"

"Why, what's up?" I ask as I lean down to put more paper in the printer.

Her expression turns serious. "They're keeping a closer

eye on Caleb. They're seeing if his dad will get tested to be a donor. Allie isn't a match."

It's not fair for a three-year-old to need a kidney transplant. "Do they think it's hereditary? From his dad's side?"

She nods. "It's looking that way. Hopefully he'll do the right thing and at least get tested."

I know that hope will go nowhere and it fills me with rage. "Are you kidding me right now? He's done nothing to help Allie. Hasn't even ever acknowledged that he has a son or paid a penny in child support. Let's not hold our breath. I'll get tested, too. We don't need anything from that guy. I do not like him, not one bit."

"I'm going to try and fly out next week to help out if I can. She's having a hard time with missing work from taking him to appointments."

"I'll call her tonight." I wish Allie and Caleb lived closer so we could help her more. I hate the thought of her being alone while she's so far away, dealing with having a sick kid as a single mom. I feel like it's partly my fault. She followed me out to California when I first got stationed there. I moved back a little over a year ago to take care of the inn after our dad died, but she hasn't been able to move back yet.

My mom nods. "It'll be okay. It's days like these I wish your dad was here. I miss him. He always knew what to say and do."

"I miss him too, Mom. If you need anything, just let me know." I give her a hug and kiss the top of her head.

"I'm just glad you're here. I know running the inn wasn't what you thought you'd be doing with your life. You need to get out more and see friends. Maybe play with your old band." She pats my arm. "Do something for yourself."

I pinch my lips together and let out a big sigh. If only it was that easy. I want to be happy here... I'm just so overwhelmed. Everything and everyone I love is struggling, between the inn and now my nephew's health. I don't know how to be happy anymore when I feel like everything around me is falling apart.

"Night, Mom," I say as I finish up and head out.

I call Sam on my way out to my cottage.

"Sam's Towing," he answers. There's loud music in the background. Friday night means he's probably at the bar playing with his band.

"Hey, it's Evan. I need a favor."

"What's up, my man? What do you need?"

"There's a green Subaru SUV broken down on Childers Highway, not far from the inn. Can you pick it up and take a look at it?"

"Sure, I can bring it in, but I'm pretty backed up at the shop. I probably can't deal with it until Monday, Tuesday at the latest, though—that okay?"

"Actually, take your time," I tell him. "She's a guest but

also helping us out. The longer you keep the car, the longer she stays, and we really need her help."

"Found another one, huh? You have a strange way of getting employees, dude."

I roll my eyes. "I'm just grateful we have such great staff right now." That's one thing I don't have to worry about.

"Any chance you're up for playing next Saturday at McGuiness tavern?" Sam asks. "We could really use someone on guitar and vocals."

I scratch my beard and open the door to my cottage. "It's been a while."

Allie and I used to play with Sam and his band at the tavern, local weddings, and parties on and off in and after high school. We started out as kids practicing in the garden shed, and probably drove my parents and guests nuts with all the noise. We actually grew into a pretty great band over the years and had a lot of fun with it. We stopped playing with them when I joined the Marines and Allie followed me to California. We've gotten together for fun sometimes when I've been on leave, but it's been several years since the last gig.

"I guess I could use some practice."

"Great! I'll let the guys know. And I'll get back to you about the car," he says, disconnecting.

I realize maybe my mom is right. I need to get out more and settle back into Freedom Valley. This is where I live now; it's time to get a life.

I didn't want to tell my mother this, but saving the family inn and our legacy doesn't leave much time for fun. Maybe that's my problem. I stopped having fun when I became an innkeeper.

I know how to be a medic in the Marines. Not an innkeeper.

I'm in over my head.

CHAPTER 3

Beth

I have to keep going.

I freeze as I open my eyes. For a minute, I forget where I am, but I'm thankful to not be sleeping in my car. It's been getting colder. Lying in this big four-poster antique bed with crisp white linens and a soft navy duvet feels so warm and cozy. I'll take this any day over a sleeping bag in my backseat, wondering if where I've stopped is safe.

I sit up and stretch, looking around the room. If I can work here for a while for free room and board until I can figure out my next move and my next book, maybe things will work out for me.

My phone buzzes. It's my agent Logan, who is also my best friend. "I hope you have some good news for me," I tell him. "I could really use some good news right now."

"I wish I did. I'm sorry. I talked with the publishers again. They just aren't interested in pursuing a contract with you if you aren't willing to put yourself out there more."

"I've poured myself into my writing. You said it was good."

"It's not your writing. Your manuscripts are amazing. But you being a recluse means the deal's dead in the water." He pauses and sighs. "I'm sorry. I know that isn't what you wanted to hear."

I bite my lip and look out at the white-capped mountain in the distance. I think about what he's asking of me, but it just feels so damn heavy. I don't want to be a public figure and I don't want to share my pain with the world. Hell no. If I share myself, people will find out what happened to me. I just can't relive all of that.

"Where are you right now? You know you can come stay with me in Boston for as long as you need."

I take a deep breath and sigh. "I'm in Freedom Valley, New Hampshire. My car broke down last night and I'm staying at an inn here. The owners said I could work for room and board until I figure out my next move."

"Work doing what?" he asks. There's a protective tone in his voice.

"Front desk manager and helping in the dining room."

"That actually might not be a bad idea. You're not too far from me; I can come up and see you. Why don't you just relax for a while and see how you feel about this in another week or so? If you're willing to be public, I'm confident I can get you a deal. You wouldn't have to worry about income for a while, Beth. This could set you up and be a great move for you."

I had a book deal and it brings in some royalties, but it hasn't done as well as it could have if I had put myself out there more. I know it and he knows it. It makes sense.

"That's what I'm going to try." I tuck my hair behind my ears. "I don't know what else to do. I'm tired, Logan. I'm tired of being on the move all the time. I need to find somewhere to settle down so I can do what I love, which is write my books."

"I know you've got some hard decisions to make, Beth, but I'm here for you. Cara, too."

"I know, thank you. I need to call Cara and check in to let her know where I am. She worries when I don't."

Cara is my other friend. She and I went to high school together in Austin. I was a foster kid, in and out of over a dozen homes from the time I was six until I aged out of the system in October of my senior year of high school. Cara and her family took me in and let me live with them until I graduated high school. We've been through a lot. Cara, her family, and Logan are all I have now.

"So, what's the inn like?" he asks, knowing he's made his point and changing the subject.

"It's really beautiful. The fact that they're willing to put me up in exchange for work is a miracle. I'm pretty sure they feel sorry for me. Heck, I feel sorry for myself. I'm a freaking trainwreck right now."

I used to be organized. I was a teacher and managed twenty-five kindergarteners every day. I had a family. I was never well-off, but I had money for groceries and a comfortable home. This is not how my life was supposed to be.

"How did I get here, Logan?" I wonder out loud.

"You've been through some hard stuff. Some serious, bad stuff. And you haven't ever taken the time to properly grieve and process. You need to stop running and deal with everything so you can move on. And I know that has to be so hard for you, but you have to do it."

"I can't just forget, Logan," I whisper.

"Yeah, but you can't keep punishing yourself for living either," he says quietly. "I love you, Beth. You know that. Whenever you're ready to deal with this, I am here. Cara is here. You have us. Always."

"I know. Thank you. I'm trying. I know I need that book deal. I'll think about it. Right now, I'm just not ready."

One thing about staying somewhere new and having the distraction of a new job is that I can think about what I want and where I'm going and figure out a plan from there. This can't be it for me. I need to find happiness again, and this might be the place that gives me a break to figure out how to get back to that. I can work, hike, get inspired, and find a new path.

I pause for a moment before adding, "But no promises."

"I'll come up and see you in a few weeks. I have some time off coming up and New Hampshire in the fall sounds like a nice way to spend it. Now you have me curious about this inn."

"That sounds good. In the meantime, I'm going to keep working on this book. Whether a publisher buys it or not, I'll keep writing. Thanks, Logan."

"Sounds good. Talk soon, B," he says then hangs up.

I grudgingly get out of bed and into the shower. A deal is a deal, and it's time for me to live up to my end of it.

I put on my favorite grey sweater, nicer jeans, and my Converse, and pull my hair back into a high ponytail, hoping this is good enough. I don't have a lot of clothes with me, or the energy to try harder. This will have to do.

CHAPTER 4

Wait, what did I
just agree to?

I wake up early and head out for a run, needing to clear my head. I've been feeling anxious since a phone call I had with the bank yesterday. I've had all this stress and pent-up energy lately.

My dad managed the inn like he was made for the job. No one could have imagined he'd have a sudden heart attack and be gone so unexpectedly. It's been almost two years now, but he left a gaping hole when he died. Everyone misses him.

My mom asked me to come help out when my tour ended.

I left California to do something I had no idea how to do. Need a combat medic? I'm your guy. Need an innkeeper to entertain and be friendly to strangers constantly? I'm not your guy.

I grew up here so you'd think it would come easily to me, but I'm still trying to figure out my place. I used to help out regularly as a kid with chores and stuff, but I never had to work with money on the business side or deal with people at the front desk. My parents did all of that. My mom still pitches in, but she's retired from a lot of the day-to-day things.

I run until I can feel the anxious energy leave my body. My sister likes to tease me that I need to run my wiggles out, just like my nephew. She's probably not wrong.

I head up the back stairs and into the kitchen. I pause when I see Beth sitting with my mom at the counter and Sasha cooking at the stove. They're laughing at something, and for a brief moment, I notice an unguarded look on Beth's face, but it quickly disappears and the wall goes back up. What is that about?

"Hey, ladies," I say as I head over to my mom. I ask Beth, "How did you sleep?"

"Great, thank you." She focuses on her coffee mug like it's the most interesting thing in the room.

I pour myself a cup of coffee and glance back at Beth. She quickly looks away and turns her focus to a half-eaten pumpkin scone on the plate in front of her. I study her face and wonder what she's thinking. She looks nervous, and I can't help but wonder if I am making her feel that way. She definitely doesn't make me nervous. I want to get to know her more. I want to know where she's been, what brought her here, and why she's living in her car.

She raises her eyes to find me watching her and quickly looks away again. Yep. She likes me. *Yes!*

My mom glances over at me. "Did you hear me?" she asks.

I shake out of my stare. "Yeah," I lie.

"Oh, good!" My mom claps her hands together excitedly.

"Wait, what did I just agree to?" I speak into my coffee cup, my eyes darting over to Sasha who's grinning while she chops up vegetables.

"You just agreed to host a fall festival here at the inn," Sasha says, clapping me on the back. She pulls open a drawer and takes out a few spices.

I swallow and look up to the ceiling. What have I just walked into? I'm not good at planning things like that. I'm still trying to figure out how to run this inn, and I'm not looking to add any more to my plate right now.

I glance over at Beth, her lips slightly parted as she takes in my reaction. She has a captivating smile. We stare at each other, neither of us looking away for what seems like a long time. Finally, she looks down, smoothing her sweater and straightening her legs under the table.

Wow. I can't remember the last time I had a connection like this with someone. I can't explain it, but she draws me in somehow. It makes me question if she feels it, too? I really think she does.

"Maybe Beth can help us?" I say, tipping my cup in her direction then taking a sip. "I bet she's great at planning festivals." I give her a subtle, playful head tilt. "What do you say? How long can you stay in Freedom Valley?"

Beth's eyes reach mine again and her gaze drifts down to my shoulders and arms. She's totally checking me out. She jerks her chin up. "It depends on my car." She twists her hands in her lap like she's nervous, and I wonder if it's me or this situation that keeps making her feel that way. I'm hoping for the former.

I haven't felt attracted to a woman like this in years. In fact, I haven't been attracted to a woman like this probably ever. I dated on occasion back in California, but never anything serious. I was gone a lot and most women couldn't deal with me not being around. And when I wasn't deployed, I was helping my sister with Caleb.

Beth is a mystery to me. I want to break down those walls I see her putting up. I want to know what her favorite foods are, what books she likes to read, what movies she wants to see, and the shows she likes to binge watch.

"I think you could both plan the festival, if you can stay longer, Beth" my mom says, glancing back and forth between us, a hopeful look on her face. "It would be great exposure locally, and maybe we can get some weddings or other events booked. I saw our schedule and it appears we have a lot of gaps to fill the next several months."

"I think I could help," Beth says. "I've planned things like this in the past. But, isn't this high season?" she asks quietly. "I thought places like this were booked up this time of year."

"It should be, yes," I say as I lift my mug and take another sip. "That's why the festival would be great for the inn. Great idea, Mom." I turn to smile at Beth. "I'm gonna go clean up, but I'll be back in a bit and then we can get started up front and talk more about this. In the meantime, make yourself at home."

I head out to my cottage to get ready for the day. The inn has just become significantly less boring, and for once since I've been back, I'm excited about something.

I run into Mellie pulling her cart with linens and cleaning supplies behind her. "Hey, Mel, how's it going?"

"Evan, hi. I need your help. Can Kase hang around up front this morning? I promise he'll be quiet. I just want to get these rooms done quickly before our new guests arrive, and it's too cold for him to play outside."

"Of course. Send him over in about thirty minutes. Or now, and tell my mom to keep him for a little bit until I can get there."

"Thanks, I owe you one!"

"It's no problem," I say, then head to my cottage.

When Mellie and Kase showed up here a few months ago, we had an agreement that, for their protection, I wouldn't tell anyone where they came from or what had happened to them. I wanted to find the person who made them have to hide in the first place and beat them to a pulp, but I knew that wouldn't help. The only way I can help is to give them a safe place to live and work. Mellie and Kase settled into the loft above the garden shed, which is our laundry facility but more like a barndominium than a shed. She loves it up there and they seem happy.

Mellie has never been afraid to voice her opinions on how to run the inn smoothly and efficiently; thankfully, she has had some really great ideas. I am grateful for both her friendship and her help. Having Kase around doesn't hurt, either. He is such a great kid. With Kase around, though, it's a constant reminder of my own family, making me wish Allie and Caleb were here, too.

I turn on my shower and strip off my running clothes. I need to get to figure out what I'm going to do to get the bank off my back. Something tells me that this festival and having Beth's help might just be the answer to our problems.

CHAPTER 5

Beth

I'm in trouble.

I'm not sure what to do with myself once Evan leaves, so I sit with Margie and Sasha a while longer. A few guests join us, but no one seems to want to linger. Everyone seems excited for hiking and other fun plans they buzz about over breakfast, then quickly leave after eating.

I refill my mug and sit with Margie. "How long has your family owned the inn?" I ask her.

"My parents inherited it from my grandfather. They passed it down to me and Richard. Then after we lost Richard, Evan began running it."

She looks over her shoulder at Sasha. "Sasha and Pete, our maintenance man, have been here since Evan was in middle school. Pete's also a former Marine. Probably what inspired Evan to enlist."

Evan was in the Marines? That makes a lot of sense. He's fit with an athletic build, and he has a military feel about him. He carries himself with confidence, and despite his neatly trimmed beard, he has a military-style haircut on the sides.

To be honest, he makes me weak in the knees and nervous as all get out when I'm around him. How am I going to work with him when I can barely form a coherent sentence around him? He caught me staring at him earlier and it was so embarrassing. I can't help it, though. He feels like coming home, which makes no sense because this isn't home and he isn't mine, but just something about him is wildly attractive. His confidence, his piercing green eyes that make me feel safe and draw me to him, his broad shoulders and massive biceps that I would love to wrap me in a big hug. I can't remember the last time I had a good, long hug.

"Kase hangs out with me most days or with Sasha here in the kitchen. Pete looks after him sometimes when he's doing outdoor projects. We've created our own little family here. And we're happy you're here helping now. I hope you can stick around for a little while. You might just like it." She sips coffee from her mug.

I take in the bright kitchen. The warm colors, the smell of amazing home-cooking. It's all so welcoming and inviting. This place is like a dream. A dream I crave and would love to belong in.

When I was little, getting tossed around in the system, I always dreamed the next place they took me would be like this. And for a while, that got me through. I kept dreaming of 'the next one'... But the next one never came close to anything like this place.

As I bounced from place to place, I dreamed of finding a real home with a nice family who would love me. Some homes they sent me to live in were really bad and some not as bad, though none were ever really good. I never felt safe or loved. I wanted a family so badly. I wanted a warm and bright kitchen where I could sit at the table and do my homework. I wanted dinner with a family and holidays with decorations and special traditions. I wanted a mom and dad to kiss me goodnight and hug me goodbye when I went to school.

"Where's your family?" Margie asks, breaking my thoughts.

"It's just me now. I don't have a family anymore."

"Anymore?" she asks, concern in her eyes.

I twist my hands in my lap. My heart feels lonely. There's more, of course, but I can't share about them. Not with anyone. It's too hard. "No."

"I'm sorry, honey," she says as she reaches over and squeezes my hand, her eyes glossy as they stare into mine.

I don't know what to say and I worry I might cry, so I just nod and look down at my mug.

I know Sasha can hear our conversation, but she doesn't add to it. All she says is, "Want to help me with the coffee bar? I put out fresh scones for the guests this time of day."

"Sure, I'd be happy to," I reply and follow her to the front desk.

The lobby has a floor-to-ceiling stone fireplace with wood stacked next to it. A vanilla-scented candle burns on the mantel, which is tastefully decorated in autumn decor. I wonder what this place looks like decorated for Christmas. *Probably breathtaking. Too bad I won't be here to see it.*

I carry the coffee carafes from the dining room to the front room along with the sugar and creamers. I place the scones under the glass dome.

As I wipe down the counters, I notice Evan strolling down the hall wearing a black and grey flannel over a black Henley shirt. His biceps are tight in his shirt and his chest is broad. He stares at me curiously and gives me the once-over. He's also wearing those fitted jeans and his work boots again. Damn, he probably smells good, too. *Ugh. Don't make it weird, Beth. And for God's sake, don't smell him. You need this job!*

He has the kind of smile I bet he could get anything with if he asked. "I see you found the coffee bar," he says. "Thanks for stocking it. Are you ready to get started?"

My cheeks flush with heat and I nervously stand up straighter. "Yes," I tell him and head in his direction.

"Having you here is going to be a huge help. Thank you for agreeing to stick around," he says as he makes his way to the computer.

"Thanks for letting me stay," I say, looking down, taking in the messy desk and piles of things stacked underneath it that looks completely disorganized and chaotic. How he can find anything up here is beyond me.

"This is going to be great for both of us," he replies, his gaze meeting mine. "If there's anything you need, just ask. I want this to work out. I know my mom threw all that festival stuff out there, but honestly, the festival isn't such a bad idea. We haven't had a fall festival since my dad died. It used to be an annual tradition here, and now I think it's time to bring it back. Freedom Valley could really use this. We usually start planning far sooner than this, but I think we can pull it off, if you're willing to help me."

Damn. I wonder if he feels that. It's like an electric shock between us. If I'm the only one feeling this, then I really need to get my head examined. He is so hot. And he does smell great, too, just like I'd guessed. A woodsy, spicy scent.

"It does sound really great, and I'd love to help. Who doesn't love a fall festival? I have some ideas, and I'd love to hear what you've done in the past."

"That's great. Okay, so now that we have that out of the way, let's go through the basics of running the front desk. It's pretty straight-forward."

Evan spends the next thirty minutes showing me the computer system, which is a dinosaur by the way, and I try hard to stay focused. He keeps side-tracking me with those electric currents that surge between us as we stand so close to each other. I resist the urge to lean against his chest and breathe him in, but let me tell you, the urge is very much there.

Evan seems okay with the guests, but there's something about his manner that makes me think he feels anxious or unsure. I wonder if it's me. It's almost like he's not confident, which doesn't make sense because he's so warm and inviting. It's like he doesn't realize how good he is at interacting with the guests and how he makes everyone seem to feel comfortable and at home. It's actually charming.

A petite blond woman comes in. She's wearing jeans and a t-shirt that reads *Support Local Farmers*. She looks like a hippie with her hair braided on both sides of her face. Gloves stick out of the back of her jeans pocket. A little blond-haired boy follows her in, waving as he takes toys from a basket by the fireplace. He sits on the rug and begins to play.

"Hey, buddy, I heard you're hanging out with me, today. Kase, this is Beth. Beth, this is Kase. And this is his mom, Mellie."

"Nice to meet you," she says as she glances at me curiously. "How long are you visiting?"

"I'm not sure." I'm hesitant to give a date because everything is so up in the air. So far, I really like it here. It seems like it's not a bad place to stay for a while and save up some money. But I don't want to be attracted to Evan, even though I can't help it. I don't think I could fight it even if I tried.

"Forever, just like you," Evan teases as he staples some papers together and adds them to a pile. He looks over at me and says, "Only kidding, but you're welcome to stay as long as you need."

Every time my gaze meets his, my heart turns over, and the way he flirts with me is really making me want to stay. *What's wrong with me?* I'm not supposed to fall for anyone. And is he really flirting with me? It's been so long since I've intentionally flirted with anyone. Is this really happening?

"Be careful, Beth," Mellie scoffs as she grins. "He might just keep you like he did us." She walks over and picks up a scone with a napkin.

I exhale. I can't imagine being needed and wanted again. I have missed that so badly.

She turns to Evan. "Are you sure you're okay with him in here?"

"Yep." He hands her a sticky note with room numbers on it. "We need these rooms cleaned in this order if you can.

Come back for lunch. Sasha made her chicken salad."

"Yum! Will do. Bye, buddy. Be good for Evan. Love you, honey." She kisses her son's head and heads out.

"He's a good kid. Aren't ya, buddy?" He walks over to Kase and musses his blond curls before kneeling to play with him.

Watching Evan with Kase only makes him more attractive. My ovaries are screaming. I want to put my walls up and isolate myself in my writing cave of a room with my laptop, but I think I actually really like it here. I feel like I can help them, especially because I'm good at planning stuff like the festival or bigger events. At another time in my life, this is something I would have jumped at the chance to do. But now? It's been a long time since I put myself out there like that with other people. When I get close to people, I lose them and get hurt.

Still, there's something about being here. I don't want to admit this, but this place might be good for me.

CHAPTER 6

Evan

How about sixty days?
That's all I can give you.

I head back to my office and close the door for my mid-morning break. It's been a few days since I've checked in with Allie, and with everything she has going on, I want to make sure she knows I'm here if she needs me.

She answers after a few rings. "Hey, Ev. How are you?" Her voice sounds tired and weary.

"I'm good. What's going on with Caleb? Mom told me about his transplant." I run my fingers through my hair as I pace.

When Allie first moved out to California, she was in college, pursuing her dreams. Once she got pregnant, she moved in with me and started working to save money. She was able to fast-track her degree and completed it with flying colors, but it wasn't easy. Once Caleb was born, I helped out as much as I could when I was home from deployments. That time I spent with my sister and nephew brought us all close together. Now, her job is what is keeping her in California because of its benefits, which she needs for Caleb's health issues. I understand why she's staying, but that doesn't mean I don't wish they could be here with us.

Caleb's father, Chris, was essentially a sperm donor for all the involvement he's had in their lives. He's never helped Allie or even acknowledged Caleb's existence. I changed diapers, babysat when I wasn't working, stayed up late with him when he was sick, and helped Allie when she was exhausted from being a full-time working single mom. She's been through a lot.

I hear her take a deep breath and then sigh. "It's not good. He's so sick." Her voice cracks and she starts to cry.

My chest tightens. "Tell me everything that's going on." My stomach sinks. "Talk to me."

"I took him in to get tests done because he's had pain and swelling. His kidneys aren't functioning right and since he's gone downhill so fast, they're putting him on dialysis. We have to get him a donor kidney as soon as possible before he gets worse."

"I'll get tested," I say immediately. "We don't need Chris to be involved. I don't trust him, especially with something this important. He's not reliable. He doesn't deserve to be around Caleb."

"He's not answering my texts, emails, or phone calls, and neither are his parents. I even had the doctor reach out, but they ignored his calls, as well."

"I'm not surprised," I bite out. "They're heartless."

"It's disheartening," she says, her voice full of defeat. "I don't know what to do. I'm upset. He's my baby, he's not supposed to be sick." She starts crying again.

"Mom wants to come out and help you. I'm going to get tested. Just tell me what I need to do."

She sniffs and says, "If you're sure, I'll give your information to our patient coordinator. I love you, Evan. Thank you."

"Keep me updated. Love you, Allie. Call me anytime, day or night. We might not live together anymore, but I'm always here for you," I reassure her.

I'm not ready to go out there and face Beth at the front desk or to be friendly and upbeat with the guests right away. I rub my eyes and take a deep breath, trying to get it together. I just met her, and what kind of man will she think I am? One who can't keep his family business together? That definitely doesn't make me look like a catch. I want to impress her and make her want to stay, not run. Hell, the stress I feel right now makes me want to run away, but I can't. I will do whatever it takes for my family and our inn.

The past two years have been awful. When I took over, the finances were shaky, but now they're downright scary. We're in trouble. We need to generate more profit if we have any hope of recovering.

I can't be the one who fails this legacy for everyone. I bury my hands in my face. *What the hell am I going to do?*

A soft knock sounds. Beth opens the door and sticks her head in. "Evan? Oh, no. I'm sorry." She eyes me for a second then comes in and shuts the door behind her. She sits in the chair opposite my desk. "Are you okay?"

"I'm fine," I say, standing. I start shuffling through my folders, trying to appear busy. "How's it going out there?"

I can't explain it, but just having her around me is soothing. When she's in a room, you can't help but feel her warmth.

"It's good. I just wanted to see if you wanted me to bring you a plate from the back?"

I gaze at Beth. Her eyes meet mine and lock there for a long while. Damn. Her kind, green eyes are comforting. She's beautiful, yet she carries herself like she doesn't even know it.

I take a deep breath and say, "Yeah, I think that would be great. I have some things I need to take care of, so it will be better for me to have lunch in my office today. Thank you."

"No problem."

After she leaves, the overwhelming feelings come back again. I lean back in my chair and link my hands behind my head. I scan my office, which used to be my dad's. I haven't been able to bring myself to get rid of his stuff. His hat and jacket are still on the hook by the door. His faded, decades-old *World's Greatest Dad* mug still holds sharpened pencils and pens and old coffee stains. If I could be half the dad he was, I'd be great. He really set the bar high. So many important and memorable conversations took place in this office. This is the very chair he sat in when I told him I was joining the Marines. I can still remember the full-of-pride look on his face when I told him.

My phone rings with a number I don't recognize. Thinking it might be for business, I answer.

"This is Hamilton McGraw at the Freedom Valley First National. I was wondering if I could talk to you for a moment."

Seriously? Could this day get any worse? I do not want to talk to this guy. He's the biggest tool, and I don't need this. Not today.

"What can I do for you?" I say curtly. I really do not like this guy. Neither did my dad. He treated my dad like he was beneath him. A typical small-town pretentious man who golfs, ass-kisses with prominent people in town, and treats other business owners like garbage. I don't care if you are a janitor or a CEO. Respect everyone. This guy is not good people. Why my family banks with him, I have no idea. My dad was big on keeping our money in our town and supporting local businesses, so I guess that explains it. Now that I'm in charge, though, things will be changing.

"I know the inn hasn't had a good go of it lately and that you're struggling, son." I try not to lose it. This guy does NOT get to call me *son* like I'm a child. I'm a grown man, a business owner. He adds, "I wanted to confirm our meeting on Monday morning. I have some very important things to discuss with you. Will your mother also be present?"

"Thank you for the unnecessary reminder. I can confirm our meeting. Thank you for calling. I will see you Monday at 10 a.m. Thanks," I say as I disconnect. I toss my phone onto my desk. "Son of a bitch."

I text Pete.

> **Evan**: Can you come to my office? Are you busy?
> **Pete**: I'm in the kitchen. Headed your way.

In less than a few minutes, the door opens and Pete enters. "What's up, man?"

Pete came to the inn when I was a scrawny twelve-year-old getting picked on in middle school. He encouraged me to take up running and taught me how to work out and defend myself when some of the relentless bullies just wouldn't quit. The middle school years were not my best years, that's for sure.

Sometimes I would ask him to tell me stories from when he was in the Marines. He didn't like to talk about a lot of it, but he did like to talk about his buddies and the brotherhood he was a part of because of it. I loved that he had that, and I desperately wanted that for myself. He's still close to a lot of his former Marine buddies, and they've even visited and stayed at the inn off and on over the years.

He was also close with my dad and always gives the best advice. With Pete, sometimes it feels like I still have a piece of my dad when hard decisions have to be made and I can turn to him.

I'll never forget the day we were fishing in the back pond and he said I'd make a great Marine. His encouragement and friendship mean everything to me. He's twelve years older than me, but given our history and us both being former Marines, we have an unbreakable bond. I feel like I have that brotherhood with him, and I don't think I'd be half the man I am today without Pete's friendship.

"I'm screwing this up," I tell him. "I feel like I'm letting everyone down." I cross my arms and lean forward.

"You're not your dad, Evan. This inn will run differently with you, but that's not necessarily a bad thing. Things are hard right now, but you'll get things back on track. I know you will. I'll help you any way I can. What can I do?"

"I don't know. Mom and Sasha seem to think the fall festival would be a great idea. We haven't done one since before Dad. That was always his passion... But now, it's overwhelming and brings up a lot of hard memories."

"If it helps, I think the community has really missed it. It's a great idea to bring it back."

"I don't know how my dad did it all."

"He didn't. He had us to help him, and we can help you, too."

"That's true," I relent.

"Well, I hear you also have a pretty lady here who might be willing to stick around and help out with it, too."

I smirk at him. He holds up his hands and says, "What? I can't help but notice that all of a sudden, a pretty woman around your age has fallen into your lap at our inn."

"She is really pretty. But she's got some pain behind those eyes. I wonder what her story is."

"That's something for you to figure out while she helps you put on the fall festival and bring this community back together. And get the inn out of the red and back into the black."

I nod. "I have a lot of work to do."

"*We* have a lot of work to do," he says as he stands and puts his hands in his pockets.

"Thanks, Pete. I am really hoping that we can pull off a miracle and get things turned around quickly." I draw a sharp breath, my gaze shifting across the room to my dad's framed family pictures. "I can't lose the inn."

"You won't. You've got this. I know you do. And we've got your back." He starts to leave, then turns to ask, "Does your mom know what's going on?"

"No, she's got enough to worry about with Allie and Caleb."

"Whatever happens, we're here for you. With you. Got it?"

I nodded. "Thanks."

After Pete leaves, Beth returns, carrying two plates. She hands me one, along with utensils wrapped in a napkin. As she turns to leave, I ask, "Would you like to join me?"

I don't know what it is about her, but I want to be around her. I want to know more about her. With her here, the inn feels a little less lonely.

I watch her hesitate and move toward the door like she was going to say no, so I say, "Please? I could use some advice on something."

She cocks her head like she's surprised. "Okay, sure." She sits on the other side of the desk and places her plate down just as my mom barges in.

"Oh, good, you're both taking a break to eat. Here, I brought you iced teas." She takes in the sight of Beth in my office eating with me. Mom's been trying to set me up with friends' daughters, guests, you name it, for quite a while now. I know she means well, but it's annoying. If I wanted to date someone, I'd find my own dates. I just haven't found anyone who interested me that I wanted to make the time for. Until now.

"Thanks, Mom," I say, reaching up to take my glass as she places Beth's down next to her.

Beth nods a thank you as she picks up her chicken salad sandwich and takes a bite. Her eyes widen. "Oh, wow, that's *really* good," she says, covering her mouth with her hand.

"Everything Sasha makes is good, but we all especially love chicken salad day," I explain. "I'm not sure what she puts in it that's so delicious, but it's my favorite. I'm glad you like it too."

"Okay, have fun, you two," Mom coos, wiggling her eyebrows then closing the door behind her as she leaves.

"She means well," I tell Beth, taking another bite of my sandwich.

Beth seems to be having an experience with her lunch and loving it. I wish I was that sandwich. I feel like I've been just going through the motions every day and not really enjoying life's little things like lunch. Beth makes me want to slow down and actually enjoy my time more, especially my time with her. I want to know more about her, but I'm trying to pace myself asking her questions. She has her guard up and I know I need to earn her trust before she'll open up to me.

"What do you think of working here so far?" I ask.

She wipes her hands on her napkin and looks at me, her

eyes clear and happy. "I really like it. If you still think I'm a good fit, I'd like to stay for a while and help. But have you heard anything about my car?" Her eyebrows draw together in worry.

Relief that she wants to stay fills me as she talks and I want to take away all her worries, including her car.

"I talked to Sam last night. He says he can look at it early next week."

"Thank you for doing that," she says, fidgeting with her napkin.

"Thank you for your help around here. You're doing great."

"What do you need to talk about?" she asks, sipping her tea, looking curiously at me.

I take a deep breath, not sure what to share with her. I don't usually share personal information with people I've just met, but there's something about Beth. I can't put my finger on it, but I feel like she's special and someone I can trust and be friends with. I decide to take a chance by telling her the truth.

"I came back after my tour ended to help my mom. But the truth is, I know nothing about being a business owner. I'm struggling. The inn is struggling. Honestly? I'm not sure I can do this." Feeling defeated, I stare down at my hands.

"I've been meaning to tell you I'm so sorry about your dad," she says. "I can understand why you are struggling, though; that's a lot of change in a small time. How can I help?"

Beth makes eye contact with me, but this time she doesn't break it. Usually, a wall seems to go back up. Not this time. Her compassionate green eyes are like magnets to my own.

Wow. There's that surge of connection between us again with her eyes locked on mine.

I want to know the secrets she hides in the shadows behind her beautiful green eyes. Why does she take a few steps forward and ten steps back? *We'll work on that.*

"What are you smiling at?" she asks. There she is. The non-standoffish one. That's the one I want to know better.

"I was wondering how long you'd be willing to for sure commit to being here. I like the idea of the fall festival, but I also need help getting a better marketing plan set up. Social media, updating our systems, and getting organized. I just don't know where to start." My eyes dart around the office and I start feeling more overwhelmed thinking about everything I need to do to get the inn back on its feet.

Happiness seems to fill her, yet she hesitates. "How about sixty days? That's all I can give you. But I do think I can help you with at least some of those things during that time."

My gaze meets hers and I feel relieved. "That would be great. I'll take it. And who knows, maybe you'll fall in love with this place. Mellie did."

"I'm serious. Sixty days. I don't stay in places long, and I don't get attached. That's all I can do." Her tone is matter of fact. She means what she's saying, clearly. How can I get her to change her mind?

"Why don't you get attached?" I ask, my interest stirred. She doesn't know this yet, but I love a challenge. So now I've just made it my mission to knock down her walls and make damn sure she gets as attached to me as I'm feeling to her right now. At times, I think I can tell that she already is, too, but something is clearly holding her back.

"I just don't. I move on and keep moving. It's just what I do," she says as she stands to clear our plates, slamming down the wall and the conversation all at once.

"Thanks, Beth," I say as she leaves and shuts the door behind her.

As a former Marine, I like the idea of having a mission to accomplish. Now I have a few of them. Get tested for Caleb. Save my inn for my family. And get Beth to like me back.

CHAPTER 7

Beth

Fifty-eight days.

I like him. I don't want to, but I do. He's annoyingly gorgeous. He's confident, beautiful, and real. He admitted he's struggling with the inn. I kept a good poker face, but let me just tell you, I wanted to come around that desk, sit on his lap, and kiss him until he forgot all his troubles. It's been a long time since I've felt like this. I miss holding hands, hugs, passionate kisses, and being excited to see your person. I miss my person.

But no. I just can't. I can't go there. It's too painful. I'm not meant to be with anyone.

I warned him that I keep moving. That probably started when I was in foster care, when I was just another mouth to feed, another person taking up space in these strangers' homes until it was time to ship me to the next home. I remember I'd find my way to a new home and think, "This is the one." Only it was never the one. No one ever really loved me or wanted me. At some point, I began to dream of building my own family instead. I wasn't going to wait for someone to want me, I was going to create it. And that's exactly what I did, until that was taken from me, too.

Don't get attached, don't love anyone. Keep it moving, Beth.

But there's something about this place. From the first time I walked up the front steps, it felt like coming home. Nowhere in the past six years ever felt like home again. Now I want to stay, badly. I'm going to spend the next sixty days enjoying this place and these people and give that to myself, at least temporarily. I can do that again. Just like I did in foster care.

The freelance social media work I've done for others has resulted in a ton of positive engagement, so I'm confident that I can help him. I didn't want to over-promise, so I didn't tell him about my background, but now I plan on overdelivering. It's the least I can do. And of course, the irony isn't lost on me that I can do social media for anyone else, just not myself.

It's Sunday already and I've spent the morning in my room

researching both inns as a whole and The Golden Gable Inn more specifically to see what I can come up with as far as a business and marketing plan.

The inn has an outdated Facebook page. They have no ads posted, and their website looks like it hasn't been updated in a decade. There isn't a way for potential guests to book online. The only way to make a reservation is to call the inn. Neither efficient nor convenient for anyone. *What the heck?*

Within hours, I have two notebook pages filled with ideas.

I look at my travel mug. Empty. I need to go out to the lobby and get some more coffee and snacks.

I throw on my cardigan and glance in the mirror. I smooth my hair back. I've been working non-stop and I'm a hot mess.

I grab my key and head out, scanning the hallway. When I don't see anyone, I race down to the front room, quickly fill my travel mug, and add cream. I snag two scones and wrap them in napkins. Then just as I turn to head back to my room, I run into a massive wall of chest.

Evan. Busted.

He smells like fall and rain. He has on a thick black jacket. His beard is trimmed, and his green eyes drink me in. Damn. This guy always looks thirsty. His arms come around me to steady me and he feels so good. I catch myself leaning into him, and judging by the way he pulls me in tighter, he doesn't seem to mind.

"Hey," he says quietly, his lips turning up as a surge passes between us, almost making me jump. "Are you hiding out in your room today?"

My eyes boldly rake over him. "Maybe. I came for provisions." I pull my cardigan in around the mess that is me. Glasses, mussed hair, and comfy clothes.

"I want you to feel at home here, Beth. You can use the front porch, the back porch, or even my cottage if you need to hang out somewhere. Don't feel like you have to hide out in your room. The inn is your home. Go where you feel comfortable." With that, he tucks a lock of my hair back behind my ear and smiles at me.

I freeze at both his gesture and his words that make my heart feel so full. *This.* This is what I've missed. Touch. Companionship. I need this. I think I need him.

He stands so close to me that I can feel the heat radiating off his body and it flushes my cheeks. He likes me too. If he doesn't and I'm reading this wrong, I'm going to get my head examined because the electricity that is charged between us is something I missed. It's like you find that person that your body and soul reacts to, whether you want it to or not. *Holy shit.*

I clear my throat and try to pretend I'm not affected by him. "Thank you. I've been working on a business plan for the inn," I say, meeting his gaze. I want to step back because the heat between us is so strong, but he's like a magnet. I can't.

He looks surprised. "Can I see?" He sounds excited.

I feel a warm glow run through me. It feels good to be needed and wanted. My love language is helping and serving people. And I haven't had this feeling for so long that I didn't even realize that I was missing it.

"I want to keep tweaking my ideas and see if I come up with new ones, but I'll have a final list of all my great ideas we can go over tomorrow and you can decide where you want to start." Just then, I catch sight of a guitar case next to the front desk. "Do you play?" I ask, motioning to the guitar.

Holy smokes. A musician? I'm screwed. Absolutely screwed. Can this guy get any more delicious?

He nods. "Since high school. Last night I played with my old friends at a local tavern." He picks up the guitar and tucks it into his office, then peels off his coat and hangs it on the peg behind the front desk.

"That's great. I love music, too."

"Do you play any instruments or sing?"

"No, I just love to go to concerts and shows, and am always listening to something." I point to my headphones now hanging on my neck. Music has been an escape for me since leaving Texas and being on the move. Before I left, I was surrounded by people constantly. Now I find myself alone most of the time. Music makes me feel less alone. Turns out so does being at the inn.

I could talk about music for hours with him, but I have

things to do.

"You should come watch us sometime," he says.

My palms start to sweat. Yes. I want to watch him play. Who wouldn't? I could watch him do anything and probably be entranced.

"Yeah, that sounds great."

"I'll let you know the next time we play."

"Thanks, I may take you up on that. I better get back to work," I say before heading back to my room.

I finished putting together a six-page business strategy plan to organize and streamline operations at the inn and I break it up into chunks to be implemented over the next two months. I feel good about what I've come up with, and I hope Evan finds this helpful.

I need a break. I grab my hiking boots and jacket from the closet. It's a little cooler here today as it's cooling off for the season. I take my phone off the charger and slide it into my pocket.

I put on my headphones and wander, taking a long walk throughout the grounds, just exploring. Leaves still decorate the trees in a gorgeous array of colors. Fall hasn't even peaked here in New England, yet it's stunning. Reds, oranges, yellows, greens, and evergreens are on every horizon, with the white-capped mountains as a backdrop.

After my walk, I head to the inn and notice an outdoor seating area with hand-carved wooden benches. Some are occupied by guests taking selfies. Families sit around the firepit while their kids play on the wooden playground in the back of the inn.

My heart feels heavy watching the families. Once upon a time, that would have been me. I shake my head.

I am not that woman anymore. This is who I am now. Nomad Beth.

I need to find time to relax here so I can write. I need to work on healing so I can finally start getting better. Heck, I'm worried about myself. But at least I have a place to stay for a while. That's one worry I can take off my plate.

I head back to my room with new focus. I might not have a plan for my life, but writing has always been my happy place. I start a new book about a girl who unexpectedly lands at an inn in New Hampshire. Write what you know? Let's see how this story plays out…

CHAPTER 8

Do you accept the deal?

As I get ready for my meeting at the bank, I think about that phone call with Hamilton. Why did he want my mom to be there? What was that all about? What's his angle here? And why now?

I head into the inn and say good morning to Sasha as I swipe a warm, frosted cinnamon roll off her counter. As I head to the front, she calls after me, "Good morning to you, too, Swiper!"

I am surprised to see Beth already at the counter, working with a guest. "Good morning," I say, wiping my mouth from the large bite of the piping hot cinnamon roll I just burned my mouth on.

"Good morning," she says, taking a sip from her mug. She has a messy bun on top of her head, and coupled with the big glasses on her face, she looks beautiful. Librarian hot as hell. I groan inside, knowing I'm not going to get that fantasy out of my head now. Today she's wearing jeans and a black shirt with a light grey cardigan over it and black booties. I know they're called booties because my sister once corrected me when she wore something similar and I had the audacity to call them boots.

Just looking at her, I don't even care that we are standing at the front desk. I want to undo her messy bun and run my fingers through her hair and kiss her until we both can't see straight.

Geez. Don't be a creep, Evan. Focus. We work together.

"You look... nice," I tell her.

"Thank you. Figured my Def Leppard shirt probably wasn't a good fit for the front desk."

"Hey, I have no problems with Def Leppard," I say, chuckling. "The inn is casual. Come as you are."

Honestly, I love her style and how she's down-to-earth. It's a breath of fresh air. She's also completely captivating and stunning without seeming to even realize it. She manages to be normal and radiant at the same time.

"What are you working on?"

She takes a sip of her mug and sets it down. I notice her eyes scanning me before she glances away quickly. *Yep. She's still into me, too.* Any sign I can get that she's into me too, I gladly file away in my memory for later. I'm going to keep track of these moments, because she *is* interested.

"Okay, I have a business strategy plan ready for the inn. Let me know when you want to go over it."

"Sounds great. I have a meeting this morning, but I'll be back this afternoon. I can't wait to see what you came up with," I say, pulling my coat on. "My mom is around if you need her, and Sasha's in the kitchen. Also, my cell number is on a sticky note on my desk. Put it in your phone and text me so I have your number as well."

"Okay," she says and nods, then heads to the coffee bar for a refill.

I keep a blank face as I enter the bank. I know if I show emotion, it will give Hamilton satisfaction. His bullying tactics may work on others, but they won't work on me. I won't let him believe he's got anything on me.

I wait in the lobby until he comes out of his glass-fronted office and waves me in. I sit straight in a chair and make sure to keep eye contact.

"Evan, it's good to see you. Did your mother come?" He

looks past me, into the lobby.

"No, she did not." I stare at him blankly.

He better make this quick, because my patience is thin and I really don't want to be here.

"How are Allie and Caleb doing? I hear that Caleb is sick. I'm sending my good thoughts and prayers his way."

I want to keep this professional, not personal, so I simply say, "Let's get straight to it."

"Right, right, got it," Hamilton draws his words slowly. He picks up a file and opens it to expose a stack of paperwork. "Fact is, Evan, the bank is calling in substantial loans we need to collect on ASAP. Your inn has a balance of ninety-six grand, due by January first."

Hamilton watches me closely. I reveal no emotion and keep my face stone straight when I reply.

"And why is this happening now, with less than ninety days' notice? My family has banked here for three generations. Is this how you treat all your loyal local clients?" I cock my head, challenging him for an explanation.

Hamilton sits back and clicks his pen. An unkind smile spreads slowly across his lips. "I don't want this either, Evan. This is just what the bank has to do, and I wanted to let you know so we can try to work something out. We can make you an offer to buy you out. I'm guessing you don't really want to be an innkeeper."

"Oh, really? And why would you guess that?"

"Your inn is struggling, and you don't really seem to be enjoying this. What would your dad say if he was here right now?"

"What's your offer?" I ask this not even remotely entertaining his idea but truly curious to what this asshat thinks he can offer.

"We are prepared to forgive the loan and offer you instead ninety-six thousand to walk away. Think of how this money can help Caleb with his medical issues and set you up in a new business to do anything you want."

I really want to punch this guy right in his patronizing sneer, but I force myself to continue to show no emotion. I finally nod and confirm, "So you need me to pay the balance by the first of the year. Is that correct?"

"Yes," he replies, shaking his head condescendingly. "I am sorry about this, Evan."

I know this man is not in fact at all sorry about any of this, and also this bullshit is something he probably takes much joy in unloading on me.

"Okay, we'll be in touch," I tell him, not giving him anything to go on. I stand and head out into the lobby.

"Do you accept the deal?" he calls, scrambling to try to catch up to me. "It won't be on the table for long and will likely decrease as time passes, so I highly encourage you to make a decision quickly."

"I'll be in touch," I tell him as I exit the bank, calling on every bit of strength in me to keep my cool and not turn around and rip his face off.

I get into my truck and calmly drive off, realizing that others may have heard parts of the conversation and well aware that rumors in a small town like Freedom Valley can spread like wildfire. The inn doesn't need that.

My knuckles grip the steering wheel as I drive to my favorite lookout point and park. I've been coming to this spot since I first learned to drive; it's my place. I get out and walk to my favorite big rock where I can sit and see the valley.

Hamilton McGraw can go to hell. I'm so angry, I'm shaking. This is personal. Why else would he be doing this to our family? I wonder if he's singling out any other local businesses right now.

It's a lot of money to come up with in a short amount of time, and I honestly don't know if we can pull this off. This wouldn't have happened if my dad was still here running the inn. I feel like a freaking failure, but I will fix this. We're not going down without a fight.

CHAPTER 9

Beth

No falling in love.

Evan was quiet when he came back and has pretty much stayed in his office all day. I don't want to push and ask what happened at his meeting, but it must have really upset him. I decide it's better to earn his trust. Let him come to me when he's ready to talk.

At lunchtime, Margie pokes her head in. "Care to join me?" she asks. I happily wrap up what I'm doing and follow her into the kitchen.

Margie pats the seat next to her and I slide into my chair. Sasha brings us steaming bowls of chili topped with cheese, sour cream, and scallions, along with buttered jalapeño cheddar cornbread. My mouth waters as she sets it down.

"Thank you, Sasha. This looks delicious," I tell her.

"How're things going up front?" Margie asks, blowing on a spoonful of chili.

"Going great, actually," I tell her. "I really love your inn."

"Thank you. I've lived here my whole life."

"What was it like to grow up here?" I ask as I place my napkin in my lap.

Margie's eyes light up and she stares off for a minute before she answers. "It was magical."

"What are holidays like here?" I ask before blowing on a spoonful of chili.

"We love to decorate the inn up big, and we have some great traditions. We have a total of nine Christmas trees that we decorate throughout the main building here. We are open 365 days a year, so we often get repeat guests throughout the holidays that don't have family or anywhere to go. Sasha makes the most incredible dinners. When Allie was here, she'd bake the most delicious pies, cookies, and cakes. She loves to bake."

As she speaks, I can't help but wonder what it might be like to grow up in a great family in such a beautiful space. Cozy fires in the stone fireplace with stockings hung. Christmas cookies freshly baked with love and set out to cool for decorating on the counter tops. Laughter, smiles, and making wonderful memories. I can see it and I can feel it. My heart longs for a life like that. One that I know I can't have.

It's what I always wanted, above anything else. Now I'm just trying to get through each day, one day at a time.

I can't stop myself from constantly thinking about my past—about *them*—yet every day I spend here, I fall more in love with this place.

Eyes on the prize, Beth. No falling in love.

I look around the inn and wonder and dream about what it would be like to stay. Forever, as Evan joked. But that's all it can be: a dream.

After lunch, I clean up the coffee bar and refresh the pastries. I vacuum and dust the front room and reorganize the front desk. It feels good to be busy. Despite getting all this accomplished, I've found time to think about the book I want to write and add some notes to my phone. It's amazing how your mind works when you don't feel so overwhelmed. Being at the inn makes me feel calm and happy.

Evan comes out from his office and does a double take. "Did you do all of this?"

"I can put it all back. I just thought..."

Oh no. I think I overstepped. I love to organize and fix things and do DIY projects. I tend to get tunnel vision and just take charge. That's what herding kindergarteners daily taught me. What if I made him mad? He looks surprised.

Damn it, Beth. You're supposed to keep your head down, do

your sixty days, and get moving. Don't make him mad and mess this up. When I was in foster care and I messed up, I had to move on. Keep it together.

"No. It looks great. I'm impressed. Thank you for all you're doing." He raises his eyebrows and nods, his eyes glowing.

Just then, the front door opens and a young couple strolls in, pulling a suitcase behind them. Without hesitating, I smile warmly and check them in. "Welcome, it's great to have you here." We make small talk about the weather and the area, and I have them smiling as they head off to their room.

Evan's mouth turns up a little. He looks pleased. I file their paperwork and update their information in the computer.

"Want to take a quick break and talk about your ideas now?" he asks.

"Sure." I gather up my notebook and laptop and head over to the coffee table where I set everything down. I refill my mug and join him on one of the sofas.

He looks like he still feels heavy from his encounter this morning, so I decide to see if he wants to talk about it. "How was your meeting today?" I ask him.

"Not good." He scoots in closer to me nonchalantly and puts his feet up on a nearby ottoman. Something about just sitting together feels relaxing and normal. My nervousness has faded a little bit, but I still feel my belly flip when he's close.

"I need to pay off the loan we owe to the bank by January first, or we'll default and lose the inn."

"How much do you owe?

"Ninety-six grand."

"Wow." I was not expecting that much.

"Yeah. So not really a good day."

I feel like my plan may possibly give him hope for the future, so I decide now's the time to share it. "Do you want to hear my ideas? Maybe there's a solution in here."

"Yeah, let's do it."

I open my laptop and pull up the plan I put together for him. He inches closer. Our arms are almost touching and the little zaps of electricity that come with that are distracting me, but still I power through. I'm excited to share everything with him.

"Okay, we're going to start by overhauling the inn's social media and scheduling out social media posts. I've created sample posts with photos I've taken around the inn and described the pictures we need to put with the various posts."

"That's cool," he says.

"I also want to put this scheduling software on the social media and website so that people can book directly online, saving both them and us time, while still keeping the inn always booked up."

As I present my ideas, his eyes widen with interest and

he nods and smiles. I can tell he's excited, and that makes me excited.

I continue explaining how the inn can be rented out as a wedding and filming venue for various types of film companies. "The idyllic New England setting would be perfect to pitch for Hallmark movies. Fortunately, I have a friend, Logan, who's a literary agent. I think he can help us make the right connections there."

"What kind of friend?" he asks.

I smile. "The best kind. He's not only my agent, he's like a brother to me." I continue with the plan and Evan seems to be thinking.

By the time I'm done, he actually seems relaxed.

"What do you think?" I finally ask.

"I think you have to stay here. If you can pull this off, I owe you big time," he says appreciatively. "Seriously, I'm not even sure where to begin with any of this. It's overwhelming but exciting."

"It is overwhelming, but it doesn't have to be," I say. "We can break all of this up into manageable chunks. I will help you."

"I'm so impressed, Beth. I actually feel like we have a chance here now."

Something about the way he looks at me soothes me and worries me at the same time. I need him to understand that I can't give him what he needs. He deserves better than me.

"Sixty days, Evan. That's all I can do, okay?" I'm not sure if I'm telling him that or telling myself that. Who is falling in love here?

"Sixty days," he replies, locking eyes with me with a look of confidence that sends sizzles down my spine. "Challenge accepted."

"Pardon? What challenge?" I ask.

"To make you fall in love with the inn and never want to leave," he says, not looking away. Something in his eyes makes me realize he isn't talking about just the inn. He's talking about me, too. And I'd be lying if I said I minded. I don't. I don't mind at all. I'm so into him it's not even funny. He makes me forget my sadness. He makes me feel less broken. And I crave that. I crave him.

CHAPTER 10

Trust me. I know.

A week later, I finish mile number three and keep going. I can't get her out of my mind. Sure, I could handle combat, stress, and physical exhaustion and still stay focused as a Marine—we trained for that—but put this woman in my inn and I basically lose my mind. All I can think about is her. My mom and Sasha love her, the guests love her, and she's doing such an amazing job here at the inn. She's everywhere; she just fits. She's comforting to be around and absolutely gorgeous. She walks around in her band T-shirts and Converse, completely unaware that she's driving me crazy.

She's still a little standoffish. I can tell she's trying really hard not to be connected or to get too close to us, but it's not working. She'll be happy, engaged, and having fun one minute, then it's like she remembers something and the light goes out. The mask goes back on. There's a pain that seems to take over, and it's hard to watch.

What would it feel like to have a woman like Beth in my life? To trust me, love me, and let me love her. Decades of love. I don't remember them being perfect. Sure, they fought, but they were an epic team. I want what they had. I could see myself making this life at the inn work with a woman like Beth. She makes me happy and challenges me at the same time. She makes me want to dream about the future. She makes me believe I can actually do this.

As I hit five miles, I start to feel tired and hungry and notice my shoe's untied. When I lean down to tie my shoe, that's when I see it: a white trash bag in the ditch, and it looks like it's moving? I walk over and tear open the bag and find two black and white puppies. I pull out my phone and call the inn.

"Golden Gable Inn, this is Beth. How can I help you?"

"It's Evan. Can you come pick me up in my truck? I need you to hurry."

"Sure, where are you?" she asks as I hear the door to my office creak open.

"I'm off Childers Road. Before we turn to go into the inn.

Do you remember that road?"

"Yes, I'll be right there."

"My keys are on my desk," I tell her. "Grab a water bottle and a bowl."

"A bowl?" she asks, puzzled.

"Yeah, for dogs."

"Hang tight," she says. "I'll be right there."

I hang up the phone and peer into the bag. I'm glad Beth can come quickly. My heart clenches as I scan the puppies and run my hands over them, checking for injuries. They're weak, but they seem to be otherwise okay. They need water and food.

"Hey, little guys. It's okay. I've got you." I take off my hoodie and wrap them in it. I pull them both to my bare chest. They're tiny and shivering. I'm still radiating heat after my long run and they lean into me, trying to absorb it. I stroke their soft little heads and hold them close to keep them warm. They're crying softly and that worries me. But, crying means they're alive, and that's what matters. What if I hadn't found them when I did?

I'm so angry. Who would do this? We have shelters that they can be dropped off at, no questions asked. Someone who wants them could have picked them up from the shelter and taken care of them. They are mine now.

When Beth pulls up in my truck and parks on a gravel patch, I open the door and set my puppy bundle on the seat.

"Thanks for coming. Can you turn the heat up?" I open the water and pour some into the bowl and watch them drink every drop.

Finally, my eyes lift to look at Beth. She's staring at me, her eyes wide as they travel over my tattoos on my chest and biceps like she's reading a map. She takes a deep breath and finally looks me in the eyes, her face reddening. *Good.* I hope she's feeling what I feel every time I see her. I've memorized every freckle on her face, the way she nervously tucks her hair behind her ear and grins when she's nervous. If I wasn't worried about these puppies, I would kiss her until we were both breathless.

"Oh, my gosh, they are so hot—I mean cute," Beth says as her face reddens even more.

I bite my lip to keep from laughing and focus on the puppies.

She slides over and reaches down to pet them. "Where did you find them?"

"In a trash bag over there," I say, gritting my teeth. I stroke their heads then set the bowl down. I climb into the truck, hold them close, and shut the door. "Let's get them home."

"What is wrong with people," Beth says, frowning and shaking her head as she turns back onto the highway.

"I don't even know. They were left there to die, loosely tied in a bag."

"I'm so glad you found them," she says, her eyes glassy.

We pull up to the inn and she parks. She leans in for a closer look. "Looks like one is a boy and this one," she says, lifting up its back legs, "is a girl." She holds the girl close and speaks softly to her, stroking the puppy's head.

"Let's get them inside. Kase is going to love this," I say as I pick up the male and we head into the kitchen.

Sasha turns from the oven and takes one look at us. "Nuh-uh. Not in my kitchen, Evan Thomas. Get those dogs out of here. I'm not getting a health code violation."

I roll my eyes but smile as we head to the front, where I fill their bowl and set it down. They stretch, drink more water, and sniff at our hands.

"I wonder if Sasha has any tuna in the kitchen," I muse.

Beth stares at me like a deer in the headlights. "I'm not going back there. She's not happy," she says, showing her palms. "You can fight her for some tuna."

"Fight who?" Sasha says, walking up behind us. She hands us a bowl of cooked ground beef. She runs a tight ship in the kitchen, but I knew there was no way she'd turn down anyone or anything that is hungry. She's a softy.

"Thanks, Sasha," I say gratefully as I take the bowl and set it on the floor.

"Where did you find them?" she asks, squatting down to pet them.

"Someone stuffed them into a trash bag and dumped them off Childers."

"Monsters," Sasha says. "You'll have to run into town to get them dog food. I can't be giving them any more of my good ground beef. But they sure are cute."

"Thanks, Sash," I say, picking up the boy and nuzzling him under my chin.

"I love her," Beth coos, holding the female and kissing her head. "Can I keep this one? You can keep that one," she says with a hopeful, peaceful glint in her eyes.

I sit back and watch her with the puppy, her usual sadness, even if just for now, replaced with joy. I want her to keep feeling that joy. Maybe this is a great way to make her want to stay. After sixty days, she won't want to leave. I have no shame. I'll use puppies to get her to see me.

"But why would you want to split them up? Don't you think you should just stay here with her?" I tease. My gaze drops to her mouth, I want to kiss her so badly.

"Sixty days, Evan." She sighs and goes back to kissing the puppy's head. Something tells me by the way she's smiling that she's trying to convince herself of that, not me.

"Sixty days to make you fall in love with the inn," I correct her as I pick up the other puppy and hold it to my cheek.

"You are a sly fox, Evan," she says with a chuckle.

"Is it working?" I ask, inches from her face, testing to see if she'll let me kiss her. Her eyes darken into bright emerald pools, but she doesn't move. Of all the moments we've shared so far, this feels like the right one, so I go for it.

I kiss her, and she leans into me, kissing me back. I keep kissing her mouth, sucking on her bottom lip until she's breathless. The way she reciprocates my kiss, her arms roaming up my chest and around my neck, I know she's into this. I start moving my kisses down her neck until I hear thunderous footsteps approaching. This is the *one* time I could definitely not have Kase be present. Little cockblocker.

"Sasha said you got two puppies!" Kase shrieks, running to us. Beth turns her attention to the little boy, but my eyes never leave her face. Now that I've kissed her, I know this is real. *I know*. This must be what women talk about when they say their ovaries ache, because she hits me right in the feelers. I'm in deep now.

Kase leans in and pets the puppies. I know just how to make his day. "Hey, buddy. Do you think you could watch them for me while I run to the store to get some supplies?"

"Yes! I can. They need toys, too, Evan," he tells me, his small voice tinged with authority. "My friend Jack has a dog and he has lots of chew toys. And treats," he adds.

"That's a good idea, buddy. I will get plenty of chew toys for them. What do you think of them?"

"I love them," he says, smiling as he pets them.

I notice Beth is smiling sadly at Kase and I wonder what she's thinking about. I nudge her and say, "Every dog needs a boy. They're going to be so happy here." I hope she can see herself happy here, too. She may not see it, but I'll do my best to show her. With puppies or whatever else it takes. I will work for this woman.

"What do we have here?" Pete asks from the doorway, looking over our shoulders. "Puppies! Aww, they're going to eat all our shoes, aren't they?"

I nod. "Probably."

"Evan found them abandoned. I think we're keeping them," Beth says, grinning. "I claim this one," she informs him, picking up the female, whose black and white pattern is slightly different than the male's so it's easy to tell them apart.

Pete shakes his head. "These dogs seem like a package deal. They're a pack."

"She's so soft and sweet," she purrs.

"You're going to have to stay here now," Pete says with a laugh. "You won't want to split them up."

This is the moment I decide that I really like this thought. "That's what I said."

Beth shoots Pete a look but he just continues to laugh. They both then look at me and I can't help but laugh too. The way she catches me looking at her mouth seems to make her nervous, but I don't miss her grin.

"Oh, go put a shirt on!" she fumes, but I don't miss the smoldering look she gives me or how she grazes my hand with hers before she walks away, cradling the puppy.

Her obvious frustration just makes Pete laugh even harder.

My mom comes back and sits on the floor next to Kase. "They will be a lot of work, but we need them. I miss our old dog, Sassy."

"Except that time he brought a baby skunk into the inn and Sasha got a fun surprise during the lunch rush." I bite back laughter at the memory.

"That's probably why she is scarred for life about dogs in her kitchen. It took us days to get the smell out and we had to comp so many nights for guests." My mom shakes her head with laughter but grimaces at the memory.

"We'll have our hands full with them because they're so little, but with all of us, I think we can get them house-trained and used to being around guests."

"Guests love puppies. This is great," I say as I rub their tiny ears between my thumb and forefinger. They're so soft.

We may have a lot to figure out, but puppies sure aren't hurting the morale around here. I think it's physically impossible to pet puppies and be upset.

I watch Beth and Kase play with the puppies, and I feel there's a real maternal sense about her. *She'd make a great mom*, I think to myself. She looks so happy right now.

"I'm going to head into town. You good with all of this?" I ask Beth.

She nods. "Sure. We've got this, don't we, Kase?" She hands Kase a puppy.

"Yup. Chew toys, Evan. Don't forget," Kase says.

Just as I get to my cottage for a quick shower and a change of clothes, Pete stops me. "How are things with you and Beth?" he asks.

I stop mid-stride and say, "Great"

"You just look really happy is all. So does she."

"I am happy."

"You deserve it. Don't forget that. You may be running the inn, but don't forget to slow down and enjoy your life, too, kid. She deserves that, and so do you."

I know Pete's right; we both deserve to be happy and enjoy life. The question is how can I convince Beth that we should be happy and enjoy life *together*?

After my shower, I head out to find Beth walking toward my truck holding two to-go mugs. "Your mom took over the front desk and Kase and told me to come with you and help you pick out the supplies," she says. "Also, I brought us coffee to-go."

I grab one of the cups and then slide into the driver's seat. "Sure, hop in."

"Thanks for letting me tag along," she says.

"Of course."

I look over at her and take her in as we ride to town. "I like you," I finally just say bluntly, giving her my best grin.

She glances at me, not seeming in the least bit surprised by my statement. She says, "I really like you, too."

"What are we going to do about this?"

"Let's just enjoy our time together," she says as she slides closer to me on the bench seat.

I put my arm around her and continue the drive into town, slowing down and savoring this time with her.

"Are you going to let me in?" I ask her, my focus on the road.

"I'm trying."

I nod and reach for her hand.

I hope so. I want to see where this goes with her.

CHAPTER 11

Beth

You like him.

He kissed me. I kissed him back. And I *really* liked it. I thought it would feel wrong to kiss someone else, but it didn't. I missed this. I had this once. I wanted this more than anything else and I lost it. I thought I could never feel this with another man. But I feel good with Evan. He makes me feel safe. He makes me want more.

And those tattoos and muscles? *Oh my God*. The man is a work of art. Literally. He's just like a whole lumberjack bad boy vibe, only he's calm and steady and amazing.

Back in my room after our ride into town for dog food and

toys, I think about what my life might be like if I deserved a life with Evan at the inn. Would he be able to love someone with my past? I shudder to think of his reaction if he really knew me. Would he pity me? It's too heavy and exhausting.

But every day I stay here, I begin to hope, and believe that maybe I could be someone's wife again… And a mother. Tears fill my eyes with memories of what if's and should have's. I grab my pen and fill a journal page of what I need to do to heal. Maybe I'll start to work on this. I have a lot to figure out. I shake my head and shudder.

As I step into the kitchen, Sasha greets me with a friendly, "Good morning!"

A warm glow flows through me. Just entering the kitchen makes me feel at home. I grab myself a mug and pour some coffee.

Margie is sitting at the table. She says, "Pour me one, too, honey, would you?"

"Sure," I say with a smile. "With cream, right?" Margie nods as I pour a mug for her and top both of ours with cream.

"That's how I like mine, too."

I'm finding a comfortable and familiar routine here at the inn with everyone and I am loving connecting with people again.

"So, how's it going with Evan?

I feel my cheeks flush. Did Evan kiss and tell? I scan Margie's expression looking for clues. She must sense my discomfort because she immediately clarifies, "For *you*? How are you liking working here?"

"It's going great," I say as casually as I can manage. I really hope she can't tell how much I like him.

Her eyes twinkle. *Welp. Clearly, she can tell.*

"You like him," she jabs, amusement flickering in her eyes.

I purse my lips and shake my head slightly, but I can't help but smile as I look away.

She doesn't even bother to conceal her delight. "I haven't seen him this happy or excited about anyone for a very long time. He's a good one, honey. He's just like his father. They protect and love their family deeply. Oh, I'm just so happy!"

"I don't know how this could work; I can't stay. I can't…" I try to hold back.

"Why can't you?" she asks kindly, her eyes questioning mine.

Can I trust this woman with my secrets? I notice that Sasha has left the room so it's just the two of us. I decide to take a chance.

"I'm a widow," I whisper. As I tell her, relief fills me.

Just saying the words lifts a huge weight off my chest. I haven't talked about this before with anyone other than Cara and Logan, and of course, they already know this about me. But to tell someone new? This is a lot for me.

Her eyes widen but her expression softens. "That's definitely not a club any of us want to belong to. I'm so sorry.

We have more in common than I thought, sadly."

I nod. "Definitely not a status I saw for myself when I was only twenty-six. Six years later and I'm still struggling to move on. How did you heal and move on? Or have you even been able to?"

"I'm still healing. Grief comes in waves. There's no timeline for it. It takes a long time, and sometimes healing just happens, like on an ordinary Saturday. You just laugh, cry a little, and exhale, because you are finally a little more at peace with it."

I nod. I like what she said about how grief has no timeline. It seems to take the edge off the guilt for me. I start to feel like maybe it's time to work through this now. Better late than never.

"Do you think it's possible to find the love of your life a second time?" I hedge.

"I do. I think to lose a husband so young is tragic and heartbreaking, but you have to keep living, Beth. Life is a gift. You have to find your happiness again."

"I know you're right. I haven't processed it very well. I bury it under my work and move around from place to place. I stay busy to try to numb out my grief. It's time to heal now, though. I can feel it, I'm just not sure how."

"May I ask what happened?"

"Car accident. I never really felt comfortable talking about it, until now I guess." I focus on the autumn leaves outside the window, trying to keep from ugly crying in front of Margie. Something about Margie makes me feel comfortable and safe. She's everything I would have wanted in a mother, one of my old foster care dreams come to life.

Margie leans over and puts her arm around me. She pulls me close to her and kisses the top of my head. This means so much to me, I bet she has no idea. I have needed this moment so badly. It feels like my permission to heal.

She pats my hand. "Take your time, sweetie. You can talk about it whenever you're ready."

We sit for a while in silence, but just being here with her is relaxing and it feels good. I haven't felt like myself in so long; instead, I've felt disassociated and lost. But being here at the inn, it's been like coming home to a home I never knew could even exist for me. It makes the grief and pain hurt a lot less.

What scares me is that I'm falling hard for Evan, but I'm falling for this place, too. This incredible inn and his amazing family. His mom is genuine and kind, I love being around Kase, and Pete and Sasha have been nothing but welcoming. Is this what it's like to have a true family, regardless of blood? I've only been here for such a short while and I have a connection to them.

"You're a good mom. Evan and Allie are so lucky to have you," I say, the words absently falling out of my mouth.

Joy shines in her eyes. "Thank you. I love being their mom.

I'm very proud of both of them."

I feel like the more I tell her, the better I will feel, so I open up some more.

"I lost my mom to cancer when I was six and I never knew my dad. I was in and out of foster homes until I aged out of the system."

Margie's hand flies to her throat and her eyes meet mine. "Oh, honey."

"I always dreamed of having a family and a home like this. Then I had it with someone and..."

A tightness fills my chest. Margie reaches over and puts her hand over mine.

I take a deep breath. "First my mom, and then my husband. I can't lose anyone again," I tell her.

Her eyes fill with tears. "I'm sorry, Beth."

I nod and try to smile. "I'm sorry for your loss, too. Like you said, not a club we want to belong to, but here we are."

She tilts her head. "I haven't known you very long, but I can tell that you are resilient and strong."

It means a lot to have her tell me this. I don't feel very resilient or strong, but hearing this from her makes me feel better.

My mind drifts off for a moment and I imagine John sitting across from me, smiling and holding my hand. I suddenly drift back to the present, realizing how much I've been living in the past and that I need to start living more for the future.

"Love is a beautiful risk. Don't miss out on something beautiful because you're afraid."

In my heart, I know she's right. I know I have a lot to figure out, I just don't know where to start.

"Please don't tell anyone what I told you. I don't want anyone to feel sorry for me or to ask me about it. It's too hard."

Just as she's about to reply, the back door opens and Mellie and Kase come barreling in.

Kase darts straight to Margie and wraps his small arms around her. She hugs him back and sweetly asks, "How are you?"

"Mom's taking me to the creek after her rooms are done. We're going to jump rocks."

"Skip rocks, buddy," Mellie corrects.

"That sounds fun," I tell him. Then ask, "Have you seen the puppies today?"

"Evan has them outside playing now. He said they needed to get their wiggles out. He also said we need to name them, but I already have the perfect names."

"What are they?" I ask, laughing at his energy and enthusiasm.

Talking with Kase makes me miss being a teacher so much. I can't teach anymore, though. I was and am still in so much pain. Who wants a withdrawn grief-filled woman for a teacher?

"Chip for the boy and Bossy for the girl." He says this matter-of-factly, then lifts the glass of milk Sasha set in front of him with both of his hands.

I can't help but laugh at his confidence in this. He's four years old and I can already tell he's so smart. I've missed having conversations like this with little kids who always have interesting and sometimes shocking opinions and who always come up with the funniest things. "And what did Evan say?"

"He said I had to check with the boss lady."

"Who is the boss lady?"

"You," he replies, now peeling the wrapper off a blueberry muffin.

Now we all laugh. Okay, so Evan considers me his boss lady. I love how he's giving me a say in the puppies. I feel like I belong.

I glance out the window to find Evan decked out in a long-sleeve, white athletic shirt that molds to his muscles *just right.* He picks up one of the puppies and scratches its ears. He kisses it before setting it down again to repeat this tenderness with its sibling. My heart swells just watching him interact with the puppies. He's a big tough guy but soft on the inside. Somewhat like the cinnamon roll characters I write in my books. Meeting Evan is like meeting the book character of my dreams.

Margie clears her throat to recapture my attention, then

asks Mellie and me, "What are you two doing tonight?"

Mellie and I exchange a glance and I reply, "Working on the marketing plan and watching Netflix, I guess."

"Relaxing with my buddy," Mellie says with a shrug.

Margie beams. "Why don't you leave Kase with me for the night and you two head to the McGuinness Tavern. Evan's playing with his old band again, and I think it would be good for you two young people to get out and have some fun."

"Can we have a sleepover?" Kase asks, his glee evident. "And bring the puppies?" Margie nods. "I'm in!" he squeals as he dances in his chair with happiness.

Mellie raises an eyebrow at me. "What do you think?"

"I guess?" Excitement washes over me and I realize how long it has been since I made a new friend and had a night out. I'm already thinking of what I want to wear and as I glance back out to Evan who is... Oh my God, is he chopping wood? Yes, yes, he is. *Holy shit.* His back muscles tense before the ax comes down and wood splitters. He stops to stack the wood and glances over and waves. *Busted.* I don't mind watching him chop wood, and I definitely wouldn't mind seeing him play guitar and sing, too.

"Okay, it's settled then," Margie says. "Girls' night for you two, Kase and Margie time for me."

I don't miss the gleam in her eyes as she winks at me.

I spend the rest of the morning and afternoon at the front desk while Evan works from his office. The puppies mostly sleep in a basket between our work areas, and we take turns taking them outside.

After a couple of instances of this, he bluntly asks, "So are we going to talk about that kiss?"

He moves closer to me, lifting my chin with the tip of his finger and leaning in close. He pulls me toward him and gently covers my lips with his. I lean in, he tastes so good. We kiss again, and this time it feels like time stops. He pulls out of the kiss but leans his cheek on mine. "I could do that forever," he whispers.

I nod, my lips feeling swollen, and whisper back, "Yep."

"I hear you're coming to watch me and the band play later." He kisses me across my cheek and down my neck. My body literally aching with desire, I lean in, wrapping my arms around him as I pull him closer. He makes me feel beautiful and confident, and like maybe this really could work.

Then suddenly, the front door swings open and I jump back as a family enters—a father with a small kid on each arm and a mother holding her tiny infant.

My eyes lock onto the baby and I can remember my own heart and arms being full like that. I know I have to snap myself out of it—of both the way Evan's kisses filled my soul and the emptiness created at the sight of this woman and her baby.

I do my best to flip into professional mode. "Welcome to The Golden Gable. Checking in?"

She struggles to get her wallet out of her diaper bag one-handed as her husband keeps the toddlers busy and out of trouble. She looks at me pleadingly and I smile my consent. She hands over her tiny baby to me. As I hold her, she immediately begins to calm. Her mother finally locates her wallet, looks relieved at both that and also to have a moment to breathe.

"You're good with her," she tells me. "Do you have any of your own?"

The spell that everything is okay with me and that I can handle seeing and interacting with babies now broken, I murmur softly, "No," and hand the baby back to her mother, then busy myself with checking them in.

I can feel Evan's eyes on me as I show the guests a map of the property and where their cottage is located. I hand the mother the keys and she thanks me as she heads out with her family. As they leave, however, I realize that wasn't so bad—at least not as bad as it has been these past few years. Usually, when I see young families, my grief comes back and paralyzes me. But Evan had me so sidetracked with that kiss that I didn't feel the usual pain and longing I would usually feel. Evan makes me feel everything good and the bad somehow disappears.

"You're good with the guests," he quips.

"I like people. I used to work with kids," I say without thinking.

"Oh yeah? What did you do?"

"Kindergarten teacher," I reply.

"You teach anymore?" he asks, his gaze penetrating me in a way that takes my breath away.

"No. I just—can't anymore." I don't know what else to say, and he doesn't press the issue. Instead, he opens an entirely more painful wound.

"Do you ever see yourself settling down and having a family?" he asks, his voice low and smooth.

"No," I say firmly, my breath catching and my stomach dipping. "That's not for me. I'm a nomad. A traveler." But of course, I'm lying. I long for that. I want that more than anything in this world. I know that I was meant to be a wife and mother. I was meant for more than this. I just don't think I deserve it.

"Okay..." he says, his eyes never leaving me. I know he's not done with this topic. I can tell he probably knows I'm lying, too.

"Okay, what?"

"Just, okay," he says confidently, then swaggers back to his office.

He wants me. He actually wants me. But the question is, will he want me when he knows what I did? Because some days I don't even want me.

CHAPTER 12

Beth

He likes me.

Later that evening, Mellie knocks on my door. She grins when I open it for her, which makes me believe she approves of my outfit. I wanted to look nice tonight. The thought of watching Evan strum his guitar at the bar with a band makes me swoon, and I want him to swoon, too. I haven't felt this way about a man for a very long time. It feels so good to get dressed up and go out. I didn't realize how much I needed this.

"Too much? Do I look okay?" I ask. I don't have a lot of clothes with me. I'm not even sure how to dress anymore to go out.

"You look great," she tells me. "I love those boots. Wow. Just, wow."

I had on black, knee-high boots in suede with a black off-the-shoulder sweater and dark blue jeans. I curled my long hair and put in my contacts, along with some light makeup and dark berry lipstick.

Mellie is wearing a boho, knee-length dress in autumn tones—brown, orange, and beige. Her brown cowgirl boots, denim jacket, and hat tie her whole look together. She's stunning without even trying.

"I love your outfit," I tell her. "I'm glad we're doing this."

I'm being honest when I tell her that I've been so focused on hiding and working on my writing and freelancing over the past few years, I haven't tried to make many new friends. In fact, I've done the complete opposite. It feels good to have a new friend.

"I never get out," she tells me. "I'm a homebody with Kase." She scrunches her face. "I'm probably going to be a dork."

"Are you worried about leaving him?" I ask.

"No, not at all, not with Margie. I trust everyone at the inn. I just feel strange not being with him, I guess."

"I think we both need this evening out more than we realize."

"I think you're right. Let's go have a good time," she says excitedly.

"Let's do this," I say, picking up my black leather jacket and purse. "Ready?"

When Margie and Kase drop us off at the tavern, Mellie quips that it feels like our mom is dropping us off at the school dance, and we all laugh.

"Evan can bring you back later."

My heart surges with the thought and I tug at my hair nervously as we get out of the car.

The tavern has the feel of a woodland cabin and it vibrates with energy. There's music playing that energizes me and makes me want to let my hair down, so-to-speak, and actually connect with others again. The smells of delicious food make me realize I haven't eaten since an early lunch.

"Have you ever heard Evan and his band play before?" I shout to Mellie over the buzz of the chatter and music.

"No. But I hear they're really good." She scans the room. When she spots Evan at the front of the room with his band, warming up, she waves and he waves back.

He's wearing a black fitted t-shirt that stretches at his biceps. The t-shirt reveals the tattoos snaked across his arms in an intriguing and complicated pattern I'd like to trace with my fingertips. I'm in another world watching him, thinking about him wrapping those strong arms around me, making me feel protected. He's only kissed me twice and I already want more.

Across the room, his green eyes stand out against his dark

hair and neatly trimmed beard. His head lowers as he begins to strum on his guitar, his fingers gliding over the strings, which makes me imagine what that would feel like to have those fingers on me.

His head raises and his eyes meet mine. Then he winks. He freaking winks at me, and my stomach dips. I smile and wave.

"I'm excited to see him play," I say to Mellie as we slide into a high top table by the bar. The server comes by and hands us menus. "I'll be right back to take your order," she tells us.

"I'm starving," Mellie says. "How about you?"

"Definitely could eat," I say, scanning the menu.

When the server returns, we order burgers and fries. Then I order an Old Fashioned and Mellie asks for a Mojito. I can't even remember the last time I had a cocktail. Coffee is usually my favorite drink of choice.

"So, you're a writer?" Mellie asks, raising her voice above the music and chatter in the background.

I'm not sure how much I want to tell Mellie about me, but as my biggest wall has already come down with Margie, I feel much less anxious when I tell her, "I'm an author, actually. Contemporary romance."

"That's impressive." She nods and smiles, as the server brings us our drinks.

I shrug. "Right now I'm struggling to publish more, but

I'm hoping to land another deal with a publisher. My agent is working on helping me with that."

"Speaking of deals, what's the deal with you and Evan?" She takes a sip of her Mojito.

"I like him. A lot."

She nods. "He likes you, too. I've never seen him like this with anyone."

I laugh a little and shake my head. "I don't know if I can do this, though. I move around a lot."

I look over at the band again, trying not to stare at Evan. Except my eyes catch his, and the smoldering gaze he sends me startles me. I quickly look away.

"So, why are you on the move all the time?" Mellie asks.

"Well… It's complicated."

"You know, Evan is one of the least complicated people I've ever known. He's worth staying for." She takes another sip and leans back.

I think about her question, and I don't know if it's the liquid confidence or what, but I finally open up to her a little bit. "I've had a lot of loss and complication in my life. I guess I'm scared. Scared to try again. Scared to lose everything again."

She sets her drink down, reaches across the table, and covers my hand with hers, her eyes never leaving mine. "I'm sorry. I have a little bit of experience with complication myself and it's not fun."

"I'm sorry, too," I say, nodding. "But there's something about this place," I say, looking around. "It feels different here. Like a good place to come and heal."

"It is different here. I'm going to share something with you. And you can't ever tell anyone, okay?"

I nod, worried about what she's about to tell me.

Mellie pauses for a minute as if she's thinking of how to respond. Finally, she takes a deep breath before she speaks. "You've heard the jokes about how Evan finds us and keeps us." Her tone is jovial but I can tell she's not joking. She glances over at Evan and smiles. "It actually is kind of true." She turns back to me. Now her tone is serious. "Kase's father isn't a good guy. We left a very scary and dangerous situation, and we were basically homeless and on the run until we landed at the inn. The Harpers are very special people to us. They're like family."

"I'm sorry that happened to you, but I'm glad you're safe now. Where did you come here from?"

"I'd rather not say. But, please never tell anyone about this conversation. Kase's dad doesn't know where we are, and we need to keep it that way."

"Your secret's safe with me," I say solemnly.

"I told you that because I really want you to understand the kind of person Evan is. He'd do anything for the people he cares about. He's worth opening up to. And staying for," she hedges.

I glance over at Evan, who leans in to say something to one of the lead singers.

Mellie continues, "He's protected us. He keeps us safe. He's like a big brother to me." Then a panic washes over her. "Oh, and also, please never post anything about me or Kase on social media. We need to stay under the radar."

"I get that. I don't like to be on social media much, either. I won't post anything and I won't tell anyone. Your secret is safe with me."

"Thanks." She nods toward the band. "He likes you so much," she says. "I can tell."

I take a sip of my Old Fashioned and try to appear calm, but inside I'm a mess. *He likes me.* My drink is starting to make me feel more loosened up and relaxed, something I haven't felt for a very long time.

In less than sixty days, I am leaving. And I know the longer I stay, the harder it will be to go. I don't want to hurt him or disappoint him. Then again, why am I so dead set on leaving? This is stupid.

CHAPTER 13

Evan

I really like you.

When she walks into the tavern, the energy changes. It feels suddenly charged with electricity, like my body knows she's here. I spot Mellie but almost don't recognize Beth. She's dressed in tight jeans that make her ass look fantastic. Her hair is down in messy waves, and I almost can't breathe when I see her. Her lips are red and when she smiles at me, my chest tightens.

My heart races and I play it cool by smiling and waving, but inside, I'm anything but cool. I'm charged up like a high-voltage electrical grid. I want to go sit with her, eat dinner with her, then take her for a long drive in my truck and go look at stars. I committed to Sam, so I'll play, but my mind isn't on our set. It's on her.

I thought she was beautiful before, but tonight she's made me fall in love with her. I smile at her occasionally from across the room, trying to play it cool. Don't make it weird, Evan. My chest fills with heat and excitement, and I can't stop thinking about that kiss earlier. I'm nervous, and I never get nervous before a gig. Playing is just fun and casual for me. But playing in front of Beth is nerve-racking.

Sam and I sit at the front with our guitars and start to sing "In Case You Didn't Know" by Brett Young. My eyes gravitate to Beth and hers lock on mine; I can only sing to her because I can only focus on her. This seems not lost on Sam as he gives me a subtle elbow shove. I'm sure he'll give me shit after this.

This song is special to me because its lyrics have resonated so much for me since I got out of the Marines. I have been waiting to find someone like Beth, and now I want to see where this goes.

I smile at her and play some more. She and Mellie are chatting, but Beth rarely looks away for very long. She watches me, sending sparks right through me. Our chemistry is fire. I've always thought it was bullshit when I've heard people describe attraction this way, but now I understand it completely.

At the end of the show, after most of the place has already cleared out, Beth waits for me, chatting with a server who's stacking chairs on tables and cleaning up for closing.

"Hey," I say. My pulse skitters as I get closer to her. I scan the room. "Where's Mellie?"

"She apparently got a ride on the back of some guy named Toad's bike. I was a little leery of letting her go, but she convinced me he's in fact a stand-up citizen and a sober ride." Her cheeks color under the heat of my gaze.

I laugh. "Yep. Toad's a good guy. I went to school with him. She'll be fine. He's in a local motorcycle club, but they're great people. We actually host them at the inn every summer for a biker retreat. Best week of the year when they all stay. We have a great time, and their club does a lot for the community of Freedom Valley. There's not many people as safe and good as Toad."

Her face relaxes. I love that she cares about Mellie, too.

I lean down and kiss her softly and she leans in for more. I can taste bourbon and salt on her. "How many cocktails did you have?"

"Two. Okay, maybe three," she says as she laughs. "Can you give me a ride?" Then she covers her mouth. "In your truck," she adds as she looks at me nervously.

I stare down at her and my mouth twitches. Her nervousness is cute and sexy at the same time. I don't break eye contact with her and neither does she. When she looks at me like this, I feel like I can take on anything, like nothing else matters. Only her. Right here, right now.

"Let's get out of here," I murmur, leaning in and kissing her behind her ear.

When she slides off her stool, she seems much taller. That's when I notice she's not wearing her usual Converse—and that her boots have heels.

Her legs look amazing. I sling my guitar case over my shoulder and rest my other hand on the small of her back as we head out into the brisk night.

A longing fills me. I want this. A woman to love and who loves me back. A partner to share my life with.

I place my guitar in the back of the truck and we climb in. I start the engine and crank up the heat. She slides over next to me for warmth.

Beth's phone dings with a notification, and she pulls it out of her purse. "Mellie made it home safe."

"You look after people you care about, don't you?" I say as I lean in and kiss her again, deeply.

"It feels good to have someone to take care of," she says breathlessly as she pulls back from our kiss.

"Can I show you one of my favorite places?" I ask. "Or do you want to head back now?"

"I'm game. Where are we going?"

"It's a surprise." I stare at her, feeling an undeniable magnetism between us.

She stares back. "You feel that, too, right?"

"Yeah. Yeah, I do."

She doesn't look away as she says, "We're so screwed."

"Yeah, we are." I laugh as I put the truck in drive.

It only takes a few minutes to get to the lookout park. I pull out the thick blankets I keep in the truck for emergencies and lay them across the hood. We climb on top, looking out over the night sky, the hood still warm from the engine.

She leans into me as we stare up at the stars. "It's so peaceful here," she tells me.

"I used to come here a lot after my dad died, when I first got back from deployment. I came here in high school, too, but that was mostly to make out with girls." My heart feels full having her here with me. It feels right to be here with her.

"When is the last time you were in a serious relationship?" she asks. She shivers and I pull her closer, wrapping a blanket around her.

"Honestly, I've never really had a serious relationship. I mean, when I was in San Diego, I dated on occasion. But I never found anyone I wanted to be serious with. How about you?" I ask.

She inhales sharply, avoiding my question which I don't miss. "Evan... I can't stay here. I said only sixty days, and I meant it. I'm scared. I can feel this going somewhere, but... it can't."

I trace her jaw with my finger and run it down the side

of her neck and back up, memorizing her face. "Why not?"

"Six years ago, I was married. He passed away," she says quietly.

I'm caught off-guard; her words still me. I knew something happened to her, knew she carried a pain with her, but I never expected to hear she was a widow at such a young age. "I'm so sorry, Beth. What happened?" I ask softly.

"Car accident. Drunk driver."

My hand instinctively goes to hers and I hold it and pull her in tighter to me. "Tell me about him."

"His name was John. I haven't been able to be with anyone since. I feel a little guilty. Like I'm cheating on him."

"What was he like?"

She stares off for a while, like she's thinking about what exactly she wants to share with me. "He was a great man, a great friend, and a great husband. He coached football and he always made sure to check in on his players. You could count on him to be there for the people he loved. We had great memories, and I loved our life together. I feel like we were just getting started, and then it was just… over. Quickly. It just ended, before it could even really begin. I've been lost ever since, just drowning in grief."

I pull her closer. I don't know what to say; I only know I want to be there for her. I can tell it was big step for her to share this with me, and I'm so glad she's finally letting me in a little bit. I'll be damned if I'm not going to go all in with her and let her know she can trust me with this.

"Being with you scares me," she finally says.

"Why?" I pull her into me, gently tucking her head under my chin.

"Because you make me believe in the future again," she whispers into my chest. "A future of not running from my pain, a future with someone who loves me, a future with a family. To be honest, I'm not sure I can do that again."

As much as I want to ask her what she means by this, I can tell it's not the right time. She's already shared so much with me tonight, and I want to give her the opportunity to tell me on her own terms. I just hold her closely, patiently waiting until she is ready to share more.

"I want to tell you more, but I don't want to give you my pain to carry. I don't want to give it to anyone. It's heavy and exhausting, even for me."

"That's what people do when they're together, Beth. They carry each other." I'm not sure how to convey to her that I can be what she needs, that I *want* to be what she needs. When words fail me, I kiss her softly, and my lips melt into hers.

A shock wave surges through me as she kisses me back. I caress her face and neck with my fingertips and then kiss her ear. Her body arches for me, wanting more.

Her hands circle my neck and she runs her fingers through my hair. I pull her closer to me as my hands skim down the curves of her body. I cup her bottom, pulling her toward me, feeling her body pulse through mine.

I pull back and she takes a deep breath.

"I really like you," she says, staring longingly at me.

"I really like you back."

My gaze falls to her luscious neck, and I go in for another kiss.

"I don't want to rush this, though," she murmurs into my lips. "I'm still trying to heal and figure things out on my own, and I don't want to rush before I'm ready."

I lean back, trying not to show how disappointed I feel but also understanding where she's coming from. I feel like we made a lot of progress tonight with her finally letting me in. Briefly, but I'll take what I can get.

"Okay," I whisper. "Let's head back."

Beth's gaze meets mine, a combination of pure desire and sadness emanating in her eyes. "Okay," she says and climbs into the truck.

She's so hot and cold, but at least we're getting warmer before we go back to cold. She's worth it; I can feel it. I'll chip away until she starts to trust me and fully lets me in.

CHAPTER 14

Beth

I'll take what I can get.

I shut the door to my room, lean back, and sink to the floor. I'm falling for him, and it's bad. Or at least, it *feels* bad. I promised myself sixty days only, and this new ripple is not going to get in the way of my leaving. Or is it? Why am I doing this to myself?

I check my phone. It's too late in Austin to call Cara. She's probably already in bed.

Ugh. What am I even doing here? This was not part of the plan. No falling in love. No getting attached. Keep moving. Why can't I keep it together?

I take out my notebook and make a list to help me sort out everything that's going on in my scattered mind.

Call Sam and ask about my car.

Go over my finances, make a firmer budget.

Get a part-time job in town in the evening?

I consider the last one. Getting away from the inn could keep me from falling for Evan...

I need to be careful. He's amazing; he's hot and kind and exactly the guy I'd fall for if I wasn't so broken. The problem is that I feel myself falling already.

I'm hoping if I keep him at arms' length and leave after the agreed-upon sixty days, I will protect us both from a future of pain and hurt. Everything I touch breaks, at least that's how I feel. Someday, I know he'll understand this.

I fall asleep dreaming of Evan and wondering what it would feel like to fall asleep with him holding me.

When I wake up the next morning, I reach for my phone. I realize I've actually slept in. I hear a knock, and without thinking, I open the door to find Evan leaning against the door jam.

My eyes widen. "Oh, no," I say before I quickly run and dive back under the covers again. Evan lets himself in. He's in a good mood.

"No! You can't see me like this! I just woke up. I'm a mess. I don't even have pants on!" I shriek, embarrassed.

He laughs. "I come bearing gifts." He pulls a cart in behind him with an assortment of breakfast treats and a coffee carafe.

"Are you trying to get into my pants? Coffee and food are how you get into my pants," I joke.

His eyes widen but then he laughs again. "But you're not wearing any pants..."

"Ugh, you know what I mean."

"Okay, noted," he says, his tone teasing. "Look, you missed breakfast, so I figured I'd bring you something to eat. I wanted to do something nice for you."

He pours coffee into a mug and adds cream to the top. He places it down on my bedside table.

I poke my head out from under the covers in time to see a pillow come sailing at my face. I duck back under for a moment to avoid the pillow crashing into me, but I force myself out of hiding to get my desperately-needed cup of coffee.

"How do you know how I take my coffee?" I ask, eyeing the mug suspiciously.

"I pay attention," he says.

My heart warms hearing that. I am still not standing up from under these covers, though. The first issue is the no pants situation. But also, I so badly want to kiss him, and if

I stand up, I might just make the move, but I haven't even brushed my teeth.

"It's time to get up," he says. "You're sleeping away one of my precious sixty days. I haven't made you fall in love with New Hampshire yet. I'm committed to that. It's time to go explore. We're going on a hike, dress comfortably and be ready in ten minutes."

"Ten minutes? Are you out of your mind? I need at least twenty. Probably thirty." I thrust my arm out from under the comforter to grab my coffee.

"Fine, nine now," he says, tone playful. "Better get moving."

I sit up, now really wishing I'd gotten up earlier and called Cara. I need to talk to her about all of this. She would know what to say.

But with only eight minutes left, I get up, take a quick shower, and pull on jeans, a t-shirt, a flannel, and my comfy hiking boots before I head out.

I don't see Evan when I get to the front, but I do see Kase and Margie playing with the puppies.

"Good morning," I tell them as I approach.

"Hey, honey. Did you have fun last night?" Margie asks.

"Yes, a lot of fun," I reply. Truthfully, it was the best night I've had in years. "How about you guys?" I bend down to tussle Kase's hair and pet the puppies. A sting hits me in the heart every time I'm around him, but it's becoming a little easier every day. I shake my gloomy thoughts away and focus instead on the conversation.

"Good. We always have a good time together. And now with these puppies? Never a dull moment."

"They're pretty great. Evan and I are going on a hike, apparently," I say, grinning. "A hike I just found out about a few minutes ago. I better get out there. See you guys tonight."

"Sasha's making the ultimate comfort foods. Meatloaf, mashed potatoes, and gravy, plus green beans and an apple crisp."

"That sounds heavenly, count me in."

"Have fun!" Margie waves as she offers one of the pups a chew toy.

When I walk out, I see Evan sitting on the back of his truck, wearing aviator sunglasses, looking fine as hell as I approach. He looks at his watch and back at me. "Twenty-six minutes," he says, shaking his head playfully. "You'd make a terrible Marine."

"Hey, I got distracted by the puppies and Kase. I can't help that they're all so cute. And it may not have been the Marines, but I had a hardcore job before this. One that even you probably couldn't hack." I kiss him on the cheek.

He pulls me close, kisses me on the lips, but then pulls back. "Teaching kindergarten is a snap. So easy," he teases.

"I'd love to see you try. You'd probably need a nap in the

afternoon just like they do."

He looks at me and deadpans, "Most definitely."

I laugh and lean my head on his shoulder. "So what's the plan for today?"

"You'll see. If we don't leave now, we'll miss out on the best part of the day. Come on," he says and opens the passenger door for me.

"Where are we going?" I ask, sliding my sunglasses and a hat on.

"A spot that has the most beautiful foliage you'll ever see this time of year in New England. Only locals know about it. Also, I convinced Sasha to pack us a lunch."

"Wait, so is this a date?"

"Yep."

"Shouldn't you just ask me to go on a date with you?"

"Where's the fun in that?

I huff but grin at him. "Alrighty then."

As we drive through town, we pass Sam's auto body shop. "Should we stop and check on my car?" I ask. I'm nervous about how much it's going to cost to fix. It's an older SUV and I can't afford to replace it.

"I talked to Sam. He's getting to it and he'll let us know as soon as he knows something."

His reply seems suspicious, like he knows something but he's holding back. "What aren't you telling me?" I ask.

"What do you mean?"

"I mean, it's been over a week now. Shouldn't we have heard something by now?" I'm starting to feel frustrated. "What if I don't have enough money to fix it? What if he can't fix it?"

"Beth, don't worry. Sam is great, he'll work with you. Today, let yourself relax. Have fun. Laugh. Take in how beautiful New England is in the fall. But first, we have one stop to make."

He pulls into the parking lot of a place called The Freedom Bean.

"Coffee?" I ask, hopeful. I raced to get ready and barely finished one mug back in the room.

"The *best* coffee," he corrects me. "You'll be ruined for any other coffees that come after this one. Except for the inn's coffee, of course."

As we head inside, the delicious fresh-brew aroma hits me and a pretty blond woman behind the counter waves in our direction. "Hey, Evan," she says, looking happy to see him.

"Hey, Kristi. How are you?" Evan replies as he leads me to the counter.

"Brought a friend?" she asks.

"Yep, this is Beth. She's helping us out for a couple of months, but we're trying to convince her to stay in Freedom Valley." He winks at me.

"Nice to meet you," I say. I'll admit, the people here are so nice, it almost makes me want to stay.

No, you can't stay, I remind myself.

"Welcome to Freedom Valley," Kristi says. "It's pretty great here, but I'm partial to it because I grew up here. Evan and I went to school together. What can I get you?"

"What do you recommend?" I ask.

"I'm loving the iced pumpkin chai right now."

"Okay, I'll have that, please."

She looks at Evan. He says, "Black coffee. Make it a large, please."

"How boring," I tease, leaning into him.

"So, are you ready to see a few of the most beautiful parts of New Hampshire?" he asks, closing the distance between us. He smells so good. A spicy, woodsy smell. I stop myself from leaning too far and falling into him.

"I am. It's so beautiful here. It will definitely be hard to leave."

He pulls me close to his chest and wraps his arms around me, holding me tight. "Well, that's my secret master plan. To make you fall in love with Freedom Valley and stay."

My heart skips a beat when he says this. He doesn't have to work too hard to make me want to stay; I already want to. The problem is that I know that I can't, and this is not making it any easier. Maybe I'll just give myself one day to pretend that I'm a normal Beth. A Beth who's capable of falling in love again. One day won't hurt, right?

I lay my head on his arm and look around. The coffee shop

is packed with people chattering and drinking coffee and a few tapping away on laptops. It's definitely giving me the itch to write. This might be a great place for me to come in the evenings and work on my new book. I write most of my novels on the road in coffee shops like this one, so it's a relaxing space for me.

Kristi hands us our coffees. We thank her then head back out to the truck.

"Maybe we should have brought the puppies," I say as I slide into the passenger seat. I'm already feeling attached to them and I want to spend as much time with them as I can.

"This hike would be too much for them. But when they get bigger, for sure, we can bring them. This spring, when the snow melts, we can take them all over the valley."

"Sixty days, Evan. Are you trying to make me stay with puppy ransom?" I ask him.

"Who said anything about me *making* you stay? I'm going to get you to *want* to stay."

I shake my head and groan, "You're not going to make this easy, are you?"

"Nope," he says, his green bedroom eyes darting a mischievous glance at me before putting the car into gear.

"Damn it."

He smiles at me and takes a big sip of his coffee, his eyes never leaving mine as we pull out of the parking lot.

When we arrive at the hiking spot about twenty minutes

later, I realize Evan was not exaggerating about how special this place is. "Wow," I tell him as I take in the view. "Evan, this place is... I don't have words. It's so peaceful here."

The sky is the perfect cornflower blue with the leaves in various autumn colors speckling the horizon with vibrant scarlet reds, honey golds, and forest evergreens. Giant boulders fill a part of the river below and the water shines like a gem.

Evan grabs our backpacks and lifts the straps of mine over my shoulders. "I know," he says, then plants a kiss on my cheek as he clasps the straps together over my chest.

Heat rushes through me and I lock eyes with him, feeling where he just touched me, making me want more.

"Ready?" he asks as he slides his backpack on, grinning at me. He's a little shit. He knows exactly what he's doing.

Oh, I'm ready. But not for a hike. Evan is stirring up things in me I haven't felt in a long time and they're coming on strong. I want things from him today that have nothing to do with hiking.

"Sure," I say, casually smiling, willing the thoughts in my head to stand down.

We walk for a while before I ask, "How far are we going? What's the difficulty level?"

"That depends," he replies. "How good are you at hiking?"

"Pretty good, I think. I've done a fair number of trails all over. That's one of the perks of being a wanderer. I get to see a lot of new, beautiful places."

Evan peers down at my beat-up hiking boots. The once-bright red laces are now more grey. "I believe that," he surmises. "You should be fine. Only the locals know about this one. Most of the tourists are on the main trails, but I prefer the quieter ones."

He's got muscles on muscles all over his body and he hikes with ease. I'm thankful that I'm a big hiker so I can keep up. As I follow behind him, staring at his backside, I wonder when he got all those tattoos and what they mean.

"So, what did you do in the Marines?"

"I was a flight medic. The guy who heads into a crisis situation to get survivors to safety and to the hospital."

He's a legit hero. Just hanging out in New Hampshire. Like no big deal. Wow. At least I know that if I fall, he should be able to save me.

"Do you miss it?"

"Every day. I like being back home, but I miss the rush of helping people. I know how to handle medical emergencies, but running a business? My dad was the best at it, but I never really paid attention until it was too late. Now, I have really big shoes to fill."

"I'm sorry about your dad."

"Thanks, he was a great guy. You'd have liked him. He was like a giant teddy bear who always made people feel welcome. He had a real gift for being an innkeeper."

"For what it's worth, I think you're doing better than you think."

He stops and looks at me for a minute and I want to freeze this moment in time. I have never had someone look at me and connect with me on this level. There's no denying that what we have is special.

"I think you're a great innkeeper," I say, leaning in to climb a steep, rocky incline. Evan reaches back to grab my hand. When he pulls me up with one arm, I feel how strong he is. I can hold my own on walks and hikes. This one is fairly hard, though.

When I make it to the top, he leans in and pulls me into his arms. I love when he's strong but tender like this.

"Thanks. You'd make a great innkeeper, too," he says, raising his eyebrows.

"Sixty days," I warn. I find a big rock to plop down on and take a long drink of water.

"I don't know. You may just lose your heart here," he teases, dramatically putting his hand to his chest.

"You're ridiculous, Evan."

"I know. But admit it, you like me."

I stare at him for a while then relent. "I've already told you, I do like you. But I can't give you what you want. You deserve more."

He looks at me for a long time and then says, "How do you know what I want?"

"I guess I don't know. What do you want?"

"I want to keep the inn, raise a family here, have a wife that loves doing life with me. Have fun times and make great memories. The simple life." I nod, then he asks me, "What do you want?"

"I want that, too," I whisper.

"Tell me what you're thinking," he asks as he sits down next to me. "Stay with me."

"I can't risk it," I say quietly. My stomach feels so heavy, like there's a lead weight in there. "I can't do it again. I can't risk it."

"Risk what?" he asks gently, his eyes searching mine.

"I can't risk losing any more people I love. I lost my mom when I was six, and I spent the rest of my childhood in and out of foster homes that were not families you'd want to be a part of. I wanted a family so bad. I finally had that—"

"You had a family," he hedges tentatively.

I swallow, choking back tears, and say, "I lost John, just like I lost my mom, and…" I take a deep breath, I can't tell him any more. This is what I meant by not being able to share this pain. It's too much. "When I let my guard down, I lose everything. It's better that I keep moving and not get attached to anyone."

"Beth." Through my tears, I can see him looking at me intensely. "Thank you for telling me. I want to know more about him. I want to know the good, the bad, and the ugly. I want to share this with you. You had a life with him before me. And if we do this, you and me? We will talk about him. We will always keep his memory alive and do our best to honor him. He deserves that and you deserve that."

"Being with you feels so good, but also like I'm doing something wrong. When I married him, I meant forever."

"I respect that, but I'm sure he'd want you to be happy. You deserve to live your life."

"That's what your mom said, too."

He laughs a little. "Well, she's a wise lady."

I shake my head while I try to squeeze back the hot tears that inevitably fall.

He holds my face in his hands and gently wipes my tears. He pulls me close and kisses me. I melt into him and time seems to stop. He kisses me so gently yet intensely, and I can't help but forget where we are. I bite his lower lip, begging for more, and he breaks away, moving the kiss to my cheek, my ear, down my neck. It's the kind of kiss that makes me want to forget my fears and my doubts and just *try*. He finds my lips again, and we kiss until somehow I don't feel as sad anymore.

"How did you do that?"

"Do what?"

"Make me stop feeling sad."

"I think this just feels right. And it could be fun to see where this goes."

"Maybe."

"Maybe?" he asks, leaning into me.

"Maybe. That's all I can give you. I can't promise more."

"I'll take what I can get," he says and kisses me again with such intensity I no longer have any idea about what I couldn't promise. I'm so wrapped up in the moment, so wrapped up in him, I can't even think.

Later that afternoon, I text Cara.

Beth: Hey, are you busy?

I see the three dots hover and finally, her response comes through.

Cara: No, call me.

She picks up on the first ring. "Hey, how are you? How's... Wait, where are you again?"

"Freedom Valley, New Hampshire. It's so beautiful here. I love it."

"Yes, Logan told me about that charming inn where you're staying. You sound really good. Happy."

"I am happy. But confused. I need some advice."

"What's going on?"

I take a deep breath and let it out before I begin. "There's this guy... He's the innkeeper."

"The innkeeper? I gotta hear this..."

"His name is Evan, and I really like him. He likes me. But I don't know..."

"Well, what don't you know? He's a grown-up and you're a grown-up. You like each other. You're both single. What's the problem?"

"I feel like I'm letting John down. I know it's crazy. It's been six years, and I know I should have it together by now. But I don't. I can't."

"Beth, you're not letting John down. He loved you so much, with all his heart, but he wouldn't want you to be living like this. You've been through so much. Steve and I have been so worried about you. I wish you'd come back to Austin and stay with us. The twins miss you, too."

The thought of going back to Austin makes me feel nauseous. There's too many memories there. And that's exactly what I keep running from, the memories.

"I can't." All at once, a flood of memories pours into my mind. Visions of backyard barbeques and weekend game nights. Too many ghosts, too much pain.

"Okay, I understand," she says.

Cara and I have always had the type of friendship where time can pass by and we can pick back up right where we left off, no problem. She understands my pain. Hell, she lived through it with me. She hurt, too.

"But you asked my advice, so I'm going to give it to you. I think you should see where it goes with Evan. You deserve this, Beth. You loved having a family and you were an amazing wife and m—"

"Cara, don't say it."

"I know, Beth. I'm sorry. But you have to live. You can't keep running from your pain and burying it under work."

I realize she's making a good point. I wonder if I did the right thing running away from Austin and all the memories, if I wasted six years of my life avoiding rather than healing.

"You did things differently, sure. I know this is hard to hear, but I think it's time to find a new normal and a new you. You're not the same Beth anymore, and that's okay, but it's time to decide who you want to be. And if you want to be that someone with Evan, then I think that's awesome."

I think of Evan and how safe and happy I feel with him. I think of the off-the-charts chemistry I feel when I'm with him. I think about how excited I am to see him every day. I think about how sad he would be if I did leave. I should at least try. Not just for me, but for him. For us.

"Okay, I'll give it a shot. I miss you guys. Maybe I'll think about coming back for a visit."

"You know you're welcome anytime. You're family, Beth."

CHAPTER 15

Sixty days.

I get up early for my run and think about my hike with Beth yesterday.

It seems like she's opening up more and more, and I want to believe that we've really turned a corner. She's been hiding so much pain behind those walls of hers, and now that she's finally started to let them down for me, of course I can understand why she's been so guarded. But where do we go from here?

It seems important that I make her feel safe and secure that I would never leave her. I know her husband didn't leave her on purpose. Her mother didn't leave her on purpose. But how can I get her to trust me?

My phone buzzes in my pocket and I pull it out to see it's Allie calling.

"Hey," I gasp.

"What are you doing? Why are you out of breath? Wait, maybe I don't want to know." She snorts.

"I'm finishing my run, dumbass. What about you guys? How's Caleb?"

"He's sleeping," she says softly. "I'm so worried about him."

"I know, we all are. Mom will be there tonight. And this morning I have an appointment to get tested."

"Thank you, Evan. I don't know how I can ever repay you…" She starts to cry.

"Hey, what are big brothers for? Besides, now you can owe me for life if I'm a match. Anytime I want cinnamon rolls, bam! You have to make them for me," I joke, trying to lighten the mood.

"Cinnamon rolls for life. Deal. I can do that. Hasn't Sasha been keeping you supplied with baked goods?" I can hear the smile in her voice.

"Sasha is the best cook, but baking is your strong suit, Allie. And if you tell her I said that, I'll deny it and tell Mom about the time you snuck out of the house in high school to ride on the back of Toad's motorcycle."

"You wouldn't."

"Oh, I would."

"Deal. Love you, Ev. Seriously. I'm so grateful for you."

"Love you, too, Al. We've got this. I'll call you as soon as I know."

I finish my run then quickly shower, get dressed, and head over to the main building. Later today, I'll be working on Beth's plan to help bring in more revenue. Her ideas are gold, and I can't wait to see everything come together. I'll also be planning out the foundation of the fall festival and organizing my dad's traditions into a list. I'm starting to get really excited about the festival. I think part of my hesitation has been that it was *his* thing, and it feels strange doing it without him now.

I know Pete is right, though. The community misses the event, and it really brought everyone together every year—not to mention nice business to the inn.

Beth is already perched at the front desk when I get there. I lean in and kiss her. "Good morning," I say into her neck as I kiss that, too.

She leans into me. "How was your run?"

"How did you know I was on a run?"

"Some of the guests were ogling you. It provided great entertainment."

"Glad I could be of service."

"Do you want some coffee? A scone?"

"Not this morning, I'm fasting. I'm about to head out to the hospital to get tested for Caleb."

"Oh, that's right. Wow. Are you nervous?"

"No. I really hope I'm a match. I'm ready to do this if I am."

She nods and kisses me, then lays her head on my chest.

"Which reminds me, I'm taking my mom to the airport tonight. Want to come along for the ride?"

Her eyes widen slightly as she shrugs. "Sure."

I trace her jaw then give her a playful boop her on her cute nose. "Good." I glance over at her screen. "What are you working on today?"

"I'm just finishing up something. I think you're going to like it." She opens a browser to reveal an updated website.

"Whoa. Did you do this?" I scroll through all the pictures and descriptions.

"Yes. And here's the best part," she says and clicks on a button that takes us to a screen with the option to book online.

"That's so great!" I say with all the enthusiasm I feel. "Online bookings will be a real game-changer for us. People can book any time of day. They don't have to wait for someone to be on duty to take reservations. This could be huge."

"Tonight I plan to finalize it for you to review so we can go live tomorrow. I've also created new social media accounts for us to post on and set up some ads that jump to the website."

This woman is incredible. "I really love it," I tell her. "Thank you. Did you show this to my mom yet?"

"No, I wanted your approval first."

"I think we need to talk about compensation, too. You're working harder than room and board. It's time we add you to our payroll."

She nods. "Thanks. That might help with my car repairs."

I wiggle my eyebrows at her. "This is great. We're keeping you," I tease as I plant a big kiss on her head and hug her.

It feels good to hug her, and when she hugs me back, I realize how much I've needed someone to hold and to be held by.

She rolls her eyes, but I don't miss the smile she tries to hide.

"Hey, you said maybe. And then you do all of this? Yeah, we're keeping you."

"Well, how does it look?" I ask when the doctor returns to the examination room.

"Very good, Evan, very good. You matched at a five, with six being the best on the HLA match score. I'm going to forward all of this over to your nephew's transplant team coordinator."

I am relieved and elated that I can now give Allie some hope.

As I walk out to my truck, I call her. "I'm a good match," I tell her.

She breathes and chokes back a sob. "Thank you."

"Of course. Now I'm going home to get Mom to the airport and then saving the inn. All in a day's work," I joke.

"What's wrong with the inn?" she asks, her tone worried. *Crap.* I realize I just stuck my foot in my mouth. She and my mom don't know the full extent of what is going on with the inn's finances.

"I'll fill you in later. We're just making some changes to the website and social media." I should have been more careful with my words. She doesn't need anything else to be worried about right now.

"That's good you're updating those. They definitely need it. So, when are you going to tell me about Beth?"

"How do you know—" I pause. "Of course. Mom."

Just hearing Allie bring Beth up puts a smile on my face. She's new and I'm not sure what's going to happen, but I am excited about her all the same.

"Mom tells me you like her. A lot."

"Beth says she's only passing through, but I'm working hard to convince her otherwise."

"Oh, geez, don't scare her off, big brother," she teases.

"Okay, I have to get back to work."

"Give Caleb a hug and kiss from his favorite uncle."

"You're his only uncle."

"Exactly."

When I get back, I find Beth and my mom in the kitchen. Beth is making up plates of food for lunch. Her hair is halfway up today, with some strands falling around her face. She looks so beautiful.

"Hey, how did it go?"

"Amazing. I'm a match!" I say excitedly as I walk over to my mom. She has tears in her eyes and looks relieved.

"I called Allie. It's going to be okay," I say, hugging my mom and patting her back. "What's for lunch? I'm starving." I scan the kitchen for clues.

"Here." Beth hands me a plate with enchiladas and a salad.

"You see this?" I say to everyone in the room. "Beth has just made employee of the month." I take a bite of my lunch, and it tastes awesome. "So good, Sash. Thank you, Beth."

"I knew you were fasting for your bloodwork so I figured you'd be really hungry," Beth says.

"Food has always been the way to his heart," Sasha adds.

"You two do make a good team." My mom beams, looking back and forth between us.

"Sixty-days," Beth murmurs. Her eyes dart over at me. But when I look at her, I can't tell if she's trying to convince me or *herself.*

"Can I tell them what you're working on?" I ask Beth. At her nod, I continue, "So, Beth designed a new website with an app attached to handle our bookings. No more old school. We can book more guests and fill our vacancies more efficiently."

"That is amazing. Way to go, Beth." My mom nods approvingly. "I'm so glad you are here. We're grateful for everything you're doing."

I look over at Beth and wink. She smiles and slides her hand over mine.

I notice my mom and Sasha gaping at us. They exchange a look.

"What?" I challenge.

"Oh, nothing," Sasha replies.

I change the subject, because I know they're scheming and matchmaking. And probably feeling pretty proud of themselves.

"What time are we leaving for the airport, Mom?

"Maybe around 4:45. What do you think?"

"Sounds good. Beth is coming, too," I say, placing my empty plate in the dishwasher.

"See you up front," I tell Beth as I kiss her cheek and head out.

After I walk down the hall, the women erupt in laughter. I can only imagine what they're saying. I did that on purpose, though. I want Beth to imagine herself staying here, because

I know I can see her here for the long run. I don't think she sees how great she is, but it's my mission to show her.

CHAPTER 16

Beth

Sometimes you need to reshuffle the deck.

I hug Margie at the airport and tear up as I watch her hug Evan tightly and whisper in his ear. These are such good people. Their love for each other and their strong family dynamic is incredible. I wish I had a mom to hug goodbye at the airport…

What am I doing here? I'm going to break their hearts when I leave. I know I can't stay; I'll never be good enough for them.

Back in the car, I shake my dark thoughts out of my head,

but Evan has already noticed something isn't quite right with me. "What's wrong?" he asks, his eyes kind.

"It's fine. Just going to miss her. And I'm worried about your sister and nephew. I can't help it." My lips press together as Evan continues to stare at me. "What?"

"You know what you need?" He looks like he's trying to be serious, but he can't help the half-smile he gets when he's trying to mess with me.

I play along. "What, Evan? Permanent employment?" I laugh nervously. His eyes twinkle with mischief.

"Well, I was going to say milkshakes and fries from the diner we passed back there, but I think I like your idea better."

"Well, I can handle fries and a shake, as long as it's chocolate," I say very seriously.

"Is there any other flavor?" he asks, his tone just as serious.

"No. And I'm so glad we're on the same page with that. Milkshakes are very important." At that, he laughs.

"You're so weird," he says playfully.

"You're the one that claims you want to keep me, and you just met me."

"Hey, the heart knows what it wants. Just like chocolate milkshakes."

We enter the restaurant and order quickly, both of us knowing exactly what we want.

"Thank you," I say to our server when she sets down our shakes and fries. We couldn't decide what dipping sauces to get so she brought them all.

"This is going to be great," he says, digging in. "Okay, we should get to know each other better, so..." he begins as he drags a fry through the garlic aioli sauce.

"Where did you go to college and what was your degree in?"

"Texas State University, elementary education." I take a sip of my milkshake and Evan's eyes never leave my straw. He shakes his head as if to knock himself out of a trance.

Now it's my turn. "What about you? Did you go to college?"

"I took some business classes at night when I was stationed in California, but it was hard to attend regularly around my deployments. The plan was always to finish my tour in the Marines, then get out and get my degree, then eventually help my dad. My taking over just happened sooner than any of us expected."

"So you always knew you'd take over the inn someday?"

"Yeah, I always pictured having my own family there. Eventually."

Panic engulfs me and I push it down. Each time this topic gets brought up with us, I can't help but question if I could even try to have a family again. Deep down, I want that more than anything; I just don't know if it's possible for me.

"Are you nervous about the transplant?" I ask, not able to meet his eyes.

"I'm worried about Caleb. He's so little. If we lose him... I don't even know what we would do. I can't imagine losing him."

My eyes fill with tears. Losing a child is devastating. I want to tell him how well I know that feeling, but I can't. I just can't talk about it yet. I feel like if I try, I might start crying and never stop and that would just be embarrassing.

Evan stares at me steadily and says, "Well, sometimes you need to reshuffle the deck. Sometimes we get dealt a hand that's a hard one. We keep playing at this game of life until the game gets better."

"But what if the game gets too hard to shuffle the cards?"

"Then I'll shuffle them for you." He brushes his hand across my cheek. "You don't have to play Solitaire anymore, Beth. You're not built for a solo game, and I think you know that."

I have been playing Solitaire. He's right. Living a life on the move from one town to the next, each one as lonely as the one before. Hiding behind writing, shutting out the world, and hiding from my grief. But now, somehow, things seem different.

"I don't know what I want anymore," I tell him. And it's true, I don't *know* what I want, but I know what I *think* I want.

I think I need time. I need time to work through the grief

that I have worked so hard to hide. It's been exhausting and I'm so tired of fighting life.

We finish and I start to feel tired. I yawn and cover my mouth.

"Want to go home?" he asks.

"Yeah."

"Come on, let's get out of here." He pulls out his wallet and places cash down on the table.

We drive the rest of the way home holding hands and I lean into him. I sneak glances over at him like I still can't believe he wants me.

"What are you thinking?" he asks.

"I like you. I like helping you and your family. I'm happy here. It feels good."

"I like you, too." He squeezes my hand tighter as he drives.

It's easy for me to forget that this is his inn, not mine. That I'm an outsider. Although he and Margie and the staff never make me feel that way. They make me feel accepted and loved in a way I haven't felt in so long.

When we pull up the drive, Evan says, "The dogs are probably ready to go out again. Want to come over and help me with them?"

"Yeah," I say. We park and walk across the grounds to his cottage.

He opens the front door to a surprisingly large space. It has wooden floors throughout and a small but bright kitchen with white cabinets and black granite countertops. There's a big leather sectional sofa and an enormous TV mounted on the wall in the living room. It's simple but nice.

I follow him over to the dining area where he keeps the kennel and hear the dogs whimpering.

"Hey, guys," I say as we reach in and each grab a pup. We bring them out to his small back deck and let them do their business.

"They're so cute," I say, watching them. We settle into a pair of Adirondack chairs. I think about what life could be like here if I could be with him. Would we have kids? Would they have his dark hair and green eyes? Would they have his dimple when they smile? I shake these thoughts out of my head.

"Are you keeping the names Kase picked?"

"Are you going to tell him no?" He chuckles. "That kid loves these dogs."

"Are you always this great?" I ask him.

"What do you mean?" He crinkles his brow.

"Who does all these things, saving puppies and people like you do? Surely you have some bad tendencies. So come on, out with it. What are they?"

"I'm pretty perfect," he says coyly as he gathers me into his arms. He holds me snugly.

I lay my head on his chest and lean into him, pretending that this could be how it would always be.

"Allie will tell you all of my faults when you meet her," he deadpans.

"Well, that's what sisters are for, right?" I say into his chest. "You give really good hugs."

"You're not so bad yourself," he whispers into my hair.

"So what are the next steps? With Allie and Caleb?"

"I'm waiting to hear when they want me to do the transplant, but I'm hoping soon." I think about Allie and Caleb, alone in California. "She's struggling. She wants to move back here, but now she has to wait to get Caleb in a good place with his health before she can afford to give up the health benefits from her job."

"That has to be so stressful being out there alone with him."

"Yeah, that's why I'm relieved my mom is out there for now. And hey, do you think you can keep an extra eye on things when I'm out west?" He looks worried.

"Of course. I will do anything you need me to do," I say softly, leaning into him.

"Want to help me do my nightly check over, then sit with me by the fire pit?"

"That's a great idea. Show me what to do so that when you're in San Diego, I can take care of things." We pick up the puppies and put them inside.

After we walk the perimeter, checking windows and doors, we pour water on all the firepits that are still smoking. When

Evan deems everything satisfactory, he walks me back to my room.

"What are we doing?" I ask.

"Get your stuff. You can stay with me in my cottage tonight if you want."

My pulse quickens, and logically I want to say no, but I can't even form the words. I want to spend as much time with him as I can. I want to know everything about him, but I'm scared that I'm getting in too deep. A night with him and I might get in deeper. I don't want to leave him; I love being with him.

He must sense my worry because he says, "I have two bedrooms. Plenty of room. Come on, you know you don't want to walk all the way back here tonight."

Against my better judgment, I say, "Okay."

He's not wrong. We're pretty much inseparable now and I don't really want to not be near him. He's wearing down these sixty days quick. And judging by his satisfactory smile, he knows it.

I grab my toiletry bag and stuff some clothes into my backpack.

As we walk back to his cottage, Evan carries my bag and holds my hand. *This is dangerous*, I think. I can lose myself in him. He is everything and it's too much. There's a part of me, though, that feels like maybe this could work. Maybe we could be together. Maybe just for now, I'm going to soak up and savor every moment with him.

We snuggle up by the fire and under a blanket and I ask Evan to tell me his favorite memories of growing up.

He thinks on it for a minute before he begins. "It was fun. Allie was only a year behind me in school, so we hung out with a lot of the same people. We always had friends over here. The inn was the place to be. Friends always knew we had plenty of food and fun here. My parents loved that our house was like that. Good and safe for all the kids to be at. My parents had a great reputation in the community so the other parents never worried."

"It's obvious the inn has always been a special place, then and now. Do you think you'll be able to pay off the loan and save the inn?"

"I don't know. I think we have a shot if we can have a successful fall festival."

"It's obvious this inn means a lot to you and your family."

"I think that's what upsets me so much about possibly losing it. I'll never get to raise my own kids here if that happens. We'll all lose it. My mom, Allie and Caleb, Mellie and Kase. Sasha and Pete."

I think about him losing everything and it stirs so much sadness in me. I already know I will do everything in the next couple of months to help him hold on. To help all of them.

"I wish I had done better," he tells me.

I hug him tight. "I think you're being too hard on yourself.

You're doing a great job." I kiss his cheek.

"Thanks," he says quietly, leaning into me. "I'm so glad you're here, Beth."

"Me, too," I whisper, and relax into his embrace.

I sit there, lost in my thoughts, wondering how Evan had ever been a stranger to me before now. It seems like we've always known each other. Like we were meant to be but just hadn't met each other yet. I had something really good with John, but I didn't have *that* with John.

But being with Evan is just like being with another piece of my soul. He feels like home. And that's what makes it so difficult to know what to do. My thoughts drift off into dreams of having a life together. I don't want this dream to end.

Apparently in a real dream, I wake up to Evan gently picking me up in the dark and carrying me inside. He lays me on a warm bed. I sit up and unzip my coat and kick my shoes off and slide under the blankets. I'm so exhausted, I fall asleep immediately.

CHAPTER 17

Worth the risk.

I turn off my alarm before it sounds. I don't want to wake Beth. When I helped her out of her coat and shoes last night, she snuggled in next to me in my bed and was out like a light. She barely moved all night, and I was grateful for the time spent close to her. I love being with her and having her here, I want to soak up every minute we have together. It's undeniable that she's got my heart.

I head to my kitchen to make coffee and let the dogs out. I set up some chew toys for them when I bring them back inside. Surprisingly, they haven't been too bad about chewing on things. They nap a lot together, and they don't like it when you separate them, even getting whiney when they're apart.

My phone buzzes and I notice an email from a neighboring inn, The Bayberry. We're technically competitors, but my friend Jay runs things over there, and we help each other out when needed. I open the email and read it quickly.

Evan,
I screwed up. I overbooked and need five rooms for part of our wedding party. Check in today, check out Sunday. I know it's high-season, but do you have five units you could spare for me? Please, please say you do. I'll owe you big time, buddy. Let me know ASAP and send over an invoice.

Thanks, Jay

I throw on a hoodie and my shoes and head over to the lobby to check what's available. When I get there, I see we only have four vacancies. I realize Beth's room is the fifth on that block, and a lightbulb goes off in my mind. I email Jay back.

Jay,
We have you covered. We'll take good care of them. I'll invoice you.

Thanks for thinking of us,
Evan

It's just for a couple of days, then she can have her room back. I know she'll understand that we can really use that income, and she can always stay in my mom's cottage if she's wary of staying with me.

I shoot Mellie a quick text, letting her know what we're doing.

I head into the kitchen and grab two plates from the buffet which I fill with eggs, bacon, toast, and fried blueberry muffins.

If Sasha notices me taking two plates, she thankfully doesn't say anything. I just want to get back over to Beth.

I head back to my cottage to find Beth sitting on the living room floor playing with the puppies. Her hair is pulled up in her typical messy bun.

"Hey," she says and smiles at me, then takes one of the plates. We sit together at the kitchen counter and I pour us both coffees.

"Thank you," she says as I set hers down in front of her and kiss her cheek.

"You're welcome," I say, now feeling nervous about telling her I need to kick her out of her room for a few days. After some small talk, I clear my throat and say, "Beth..."

She puts her fork down and eyes me cautiously. "Did I do something wrong?"

"No, no, nothing like that." I sigh. "Okay, I might have jumped the gun, but I gave your room away today." Her eyes widen but I continue, "One of the neighboring inns was overbooked and they needed five of our rooms. We had four vacancies, and then your room. I know this seems presumptuous, but I was wondering if you'd like to stay here, in my second bedroom. Or, if you want, you could stay over at my mom's cottage. I know she wouldn't mind, either. I'm sorry, but we could really use the money."

"It's totally fine. You letting me stay here is a favor, Evan. I will go wherever you guys want to put me. I'm just thankful for the room and board. So, should I stay at your mom's?" she hedges, biting her lip and trying not to smile.

"Oh, you're staying here," I say, my tone empathic. "It makes sense to stay with me."

"Oh, it does?" she teases, covering her mouth as she shakes her head, laughing.

"This way you're close by for me to kiss you anytime I want." I gauge her reaction to see what she does and am pleased when her eyes widen and she smiles. "Seriously, though. Your comfort matters to me. When you first got here, we had plenty of vacancies. Now, with your help, we are filling up. I'm so thankful for you, Beth. Stay wherever you feel most comfortable."

She puts down her fork and hugs me, laying her head on my chest. I breathe her in before she peers up at me and says, "Don't fall in love with me."

I deadpan back, "Of course not. Maybe you shouldn't fall

in love with me, either," I tease.

"Too late," she mumbles.

"What's that?" I ask.

"Nothing," she says nonchalantly. "Nothing at all."

I take our plates to the sink and rinse them, giving her a moment to believe I didn't hear her. I turn around, smirking, and whisper conspiratorially, "You're already falling in love with me."

She bends down to pick up Bossy. She holds her close and kisses her head. "It will be hard to leave them."

Hearing this come out of her mouth, I wonder if she's thinking about us and leaving me, as well. We have something here; I know it and she knows it. I'm just running out of ideas on how to convince her to stay, that this is where she belongs, here at the inn, with me.

"You mean me? It'll be hard to leave *me*? A simple way to fix this is to not leave," I say as I stack the plates and silverware. "Besides, you said maybe..."

I know she's been through stuff and I'm trying to be patient, but I know what I want. I want to see where this goes. Beth being here gives me hope for the inn and my future—*our* future.

She stares at me for a long time, then says, "What would it look like if I stay? What if we do this and it doesn't work?"

I take her hands in mine and look deeply into her eyes. "Every minute I get to spend with you is worth the risk."

Later that morning, I text Allie from my office to see if everyone's okay.

She writes back right away.

> **Allie**: We're all good. Mom's already bought groceries, cooked breakfast, and is cleaning.
> **Evan**: You know Mom. She loves to help and doesn't have an off button.

She starts typing back before I even hit send. It's not only our mom who doesn't have an off button.

> **Allie**: She's a godsend. I've been burning the candle at both ends with getting Caleb to his appointments and taking care of him while working into the late hours of the night to get my work done.

It pains me that she's stretched so thin and so alone. I'm so happy our mom's there with her to give her a much deserved break.

> **Evan**: You can't do it all alone, you need help. I'm so glad she's there. Any word from the transplant team?
> **Allie**: Yeah, just waiting to get him to a place where he can do the surgery. They said they'd be in touch, but it might be a quick turnaround.
> **Evan**: I'll be ready.

Allie: Thanks, Ev. I love you.

There's not much I can do until I hear back about when we can do the transplant, so I get to work. I'm shocked to discover we've already booked out the next few months and that people have been calling to be put on a waiting list for cancellations. That hasn't happened before.

I run our numbers. We're already doing so much better than this time last year. I spend the morning setting up new business accounts for the inn and transferring money away from Hamilton's bank. I can't have that guy seeing our finances.

Beth comes by with her bags and stops in my doorway. "I got my stuff out and I'm going to move it all into your cottage, if that's still okay. Thanks again."

"That's what I like to hear. Come here," I say, meeting her at the door and shutting out the rest of the world.

I kiss her deeply and urgently. I lift her, wrapping her legs around my hips, and push her up against the wall, kissing her until we're both out of breath. I want to take things further, I know I'm ready for more, but I'm not going to go there until I know for a fact that she's ready, too.

It takes everything in me but I pull back to take her in. Her eyes are glazed and heavy. She looks like a hot mess, emphasis on the "hot". Definitely not suitable for work, but I can't help myself around her. "You might want to take a minute to get yourself together," I tell her, but I don't want to release her just yet. I hold her in my arms and never want to let go.

I'm trying to silently convey that this is what it would be like if she stayed. We'd run this inn, day in and day out, sneaking make-out sessions where we can, making each other smile and laugh, just doing life together. She makes my life better; I want her to feel the same.

She peers up at me, her face filled with desire. "Am I safe in here or are we going to keep doing this?"

"Probably just keep doing this," I say confidently, then claim her mouth again. I feel a jump of excitement when she leans in and claims me back.

Just as I go in to deepen our kiss, a knock at the door makes us both jump.

Mellie's there, arm poised to knock again. "Hey, I was just checking in. I can't find Beth. I was going to see if she wanted to eat lunch with us. Have you seen her?" I feel Beth's hand close over my wrist and squeeze, as if telling me not to give her away.

"Haven't seen her. She might be moving into the cottage. I'll tell her we're all eating together."

"Okay," she says, picking up her cleaning caddy and heading toward the kitchen. I don't miss her eyeroll, letting me know that she knows exactly what's going on in here.

I shut the door and Beth snorts. "Thanks. I was worried she'd catch us and—"

"And, what? You think they all don't already know?" I gather her in my arms and pull her close. "No one will be surprised, trust me." I kiss her on the top of her head.

She leans into me and hugs me back. Then she takes a deep breath and pulls away. "I'll go out the front and around to the cottage."

She picks up her stuff as she heads out the door, and I give her a sly look. "Maybe..."

She grins. "Maybe..."

I go back to work for a little while until Kase pops his head into my office. "My mom says to tell you Beth made your food again."

"I'm coming, buddy." I follow him to the kitchen. It feels nice to have Beth do things for me. It makes me feel like she wants me. I love to see that nurturing side of her starting to come out the longer she's here. I didn't know how much I needed her until she was here, and now that I'm used her to her being around, I can't imagine life without her. If she leaves, it's probably going to devastate me.

I watch them for a while before they know I'm there. Sasha, Beth, and Mellie, all chatting animatedly and looking happy as Kase climbs onto the stool at the counter. These people right here in this room are my *why*. Why I will give everything I have to save the inn and make this right.

I slide onto the stool next to Beth where she's already set a plate for me. "Thank you for lunch. Again."

"You're welcome." She looks over at me and smiles, and I realize the shyness is almost gone. She's more calm and confident now than she was when she got here.

We dive into Cuban sandwiches, sweet potato chips, and homemade pickles.

"Sasha," I moan into my sandwich. "These are so good. Are these your homemade pickles?"

"Thank you, and yes they are. We need to find someone to help with the garden this year. Someone who actually loves gardening, someone who is not me. I like cooking, not gardening," she says as she wipes down her counter.

Mellie's eyes light up. "I love gardening. Can I help?"

I tilt my head at Sasha, who answers, "Yes. We have our seasonal help coming back for housekeeping, right?"

"We do," I say. "And I'm also happy to help you with any gardening, too, Sasha."

We grow all our own herbs and most of our vegetables. We've talked about expanding and setting up a farmer's market on the property, but we haven't had the staff to do it. Maybe that's another way we can get Beth to stay?

Mellie looks at Beth. "What's new?" she asks her. "Haven't had a chance to catch up with you lately."

"Actually, I've been working on the website," Beth tells her.

Sasha pulls up our website on her phone. "Speaking of, Beth, this looks so good. We even have a tab for the dining room. I love it!"

"Thank you," Beth says. "It's a work in progress, but we're getting there."

I reach out and squeeze Beth's thigh under the table and she leans her head on my arm.

"Kase, you want to help me with the puppies after lunch?" I ask. "I'm trying to teach them to walk on their leashes better."

He sets his milk down. "Yep. Mom said I can pretend they're mine too."

"They're yours too, buddy. They live here, and so do you. You don't have to pretend." I see Mellie watching us, smiling. She mouths, "Thank you," to me. I nod back.

"Hey, how's your mom doing with Allie and Caleb?" Sasha asks.

"Good. We're waiting to hear more about the transplant. I may have to fly out quickly when they schedule it."

Sasha's eyes fill with hope. "It's going to be okay, kiddo." She squeezes my shoulder.

That afternoon, I head out to run errands while Beth handles the front desk.

When I stop for gas, I see Hamilton pull up and get out to pump gas into his Audi sports car. I hold my head forward, thankful I'm wearing sunglasses so he doesn't see me watching him.

I finish pumping my own gas and when I turn around, he's standing a few feet from me like a damn little annoying leprechaun. He reminds me of an angry little Danny DeVito.

"I thought that was you," he says. "I haven't heard from you. Did you still want to accept the bank's offer?" His eyes aren't kind.

I stare at him, expressionless. He looks nervous before finally moving aside so I can get past him.

I have no idea what his game is, but I'm not playing. This is my inn, my family's legacy, and he's picked the wrong man to try and bully.

CHAPTER 18

Beth

You give good hugs.

I help Sasha clean up after lunch and Mellie heads off to put Kase down for a nap and take a break. Sasha makes eye contact with me for a bit before she finally says something.

"I'm glad to hear you're sticking around for a while." She turns and starts wiping down the counters. "The Harpers are good people. They've been through a lot, but they've remained loyal and strong. Whatever's holding you back from him... I'm just saying..."

"I wish it was that simple," I say. I lean back and consider her words.

"It's as simple or as complicated as you want it to be. It's hard to love and be loved when you've been hurt. I get it. But I'll tell you, I've known Evan since he was a boy. I've never seen him like this with anyone. Ever. There's something about you, Beth. I think he needs you, and you need him."

I nod. My phone buzzes and I look down. Logan. "I'm sorry, I need to take this. Thanks, Sasha. I hear you." I give her a smile then head up to the front room.

"Hey, how are you?" I answer as I curl up on one of the couches in front of the fireplace.

"Good. Just wanted to check in on you. Cara said she talked to you."

"I'm okay. Working is good for me. It feels good to feel needed again."

"I'm really glad to hear that. You can say it..."

"You were right."

"Okay, I'm going to need you to repeat that so we can record it and play it again and again," he teases.

"Ha, ha. How's Boston? Are you settling into your new place?"

"Bean town is good. The renovations are coming along. I like it here. I signed a new client and I'm excited. Speaking of clients, how's the writing coming?"

"I haven't had a lot of time to write, to be honest."

"That's okay," he assures me. "You're supposed to be

taking a break and not worrying too much about writing right now, anyway. Any thought about whether or not you'll consider being more public?"

"I know I need to do it, Logan. And I probably will. I do feel a little better about things. I've told Evan and his mother about what happened."

"Wow, you did?"

"Not all of it. But some. That's progress for me. You know I'm not really an open book."

"Oh, I'm aware." Logan laughs. "Anyway, just wanted to check in. I shared your proposal with a few more editors. I'm just waiting for the go-ahead from you that you're willing to do more. That's it, Beth."

"I know," I say. "I'm thinking about it."

"Good. I'll be up to visit soon. I'm getting my floors redone and need a place to stay. Plus, I miss you. Cara misses you, too. Don't be a stranger."

"Thanks, you, too. I'm looking forward to seeing you and introducing you to everyone."

After my phone call with Logan, I'm feeling a bit refreshed. I know what I need to do, I just need to finally take the steps to get there. I spend the afternoon attending to guests and organizing the social media posts I've created. I also take more pictures to post. So far, the website looks amazing and we're booking up like crazy. I send a link to the updated site to Margie in San Diego and ask her how everyone's doing.

> **Margie**: Hey, sweetie. Doing good here. The website looks amazing! Thank you so much for doing that. Taking good care of them. Please keep him in your thoughts and prayers. We're heading to dialysis now.

She sends me a picture of her with Caleb. He looks so small and sick in his booster seat, it breaks my heart.

> **Beth**: Aww, he's so cute!
> **Margie**: Will do. Take good care of Evan for me.
> **Beth**: Will do!

I think about Evan and wonder how things will go later, staying together for the night in his cottage. It doesn't feel strange, even though it probably should. We've spent nearly every day and most evenings together since I've been here, and at this point, it would feel more strange to not be spending time with him if he's nearby. I love being with him.

"What?" I look up to find Evan standing there, smiling at me. "What are you smiling at?" I challenge.

"You seem frustrated about something." I smirk and shrug. He says, "You look like you need a hug," and opens his arms. I walk into his embrace and wrap my arms around his waist, breathing him in. I could stay in this man's arms forever.

"Did you just smell me?" he teases.

"No. Maybe. I don't know, okay?" I say, muddled as I hug him tighter.

"What's wrong?" he asks, holding me closer.

"Nothing anymore. You give good hugs."

"Thanks. You do, too."

I have that happy feeling but nervous stomach. So many good things are happening right now and I'm nervous that something will go wrong or that I shouldn't feel happy. I know I need to just live in the moment. It just feels like a risk because I've had the rug ripped out from under me before and I'm worried it will happen again. I know it isn't fair to Evan, though, me living with one foot in and one foot out, always waiting for the other shoe to drop.

Evan thankfully interrupts my deep thoughts. "So, I picked up some groceries and dropped them off at the cottage and checked on the puppies. Kase and I took them on a walk a while ago. Did you get settled in over there?"

"Yeah, I set up in your guest room so I can give you some space."

"I don't need space," he says as he hugs me tight.

"You might. I don't want to get in your way."

"What if I want you to get in my way?"

I pull back and kiss his cheek and then straighten up as a guest approaches the coffee bar.

"You two are the cutest couple," she says with a warm smile.

My cheeks burn at hearing Evan and me referred to as a couple. Still, I straighten up and say, "Thanks," not bothering to correct her.

She beams and whispers, "He's so handsome."

Evan blushes and says, "I have to get some things done. Let me know if you need anything, Beth. Enjoy your stay," he says to the guest, then disappears back into his office.

Once I take care of her business and she heads back to her room, I clean up the front, restock the coffee bar and mini-fridge, and tidy up the front living room. I'm folding an afghan over the edge of the couch when Evan comes back out of his office and asks, "Ready to head home?"

Home. I do like the sound of that... And it doesn't even feel terrifying. I mean, not *completely* terrifying.

"Yep, just let me finish tidying up. What are we doing for dinner? Want me to fix something?"

He looks back at the kitchen. "We can probably just get two to-go containers and hang out by the fire pit if you want. The puppies could use the outside time."

"Sounds good." I will admit, my heart feels so good and content when I think of having someone to take care of again, so I'm disappointed when he suggests we just get something from the main kitchen. I miss having someone to cook for. I make a mental note to scan his kitchen and see what I can whip up later on in the week.

We walk back to the cottage like we've been doing this for ages; it feels so natural. My hand slips into his. I look up at him and he smiles down at me. I am letting my guard down and I hate it and love it at the same time. The ease I feel when he's around is like nothing I've experienced before. I don't think I could stop falling in love with this man if I tried.

I set up our food at the table while he lets out the dogs and I get two beers out of the fridge. I light a candle on his counter and turn on some lamps. This place could definitely use more homey touches. Maybe some plants, cozy blankets, and books. He doesn't spend a lot of time in here and it shows.

Evan comes back in with the dogs and pours food into their bowls before we sit down to eat, too. I can't help but notice that he looks tense. My heart feels heavier when I see his brow is creased and the warm smile he usually wears is replaced by a tight line. He's clearly got a lot on his mind.

"You doing okay?" I ask.

"Yeah, just nervous about the transplant stuff. I wish Caleb didn't have to deal with any of this."

"I texted with your mom today and she sent me a picture of him. He's so tiny. I can't believe he's going through all of this, either. He's so lucky your kidney is a match."

"Yeah, we lucked out there for sure."

"What are you most worried about?"

"Him not making it through the surgery. Or rejecting the kidney."

"I wish I knew what to say to make it better. I'll do my best here while you're gone so you'll have peace of mind with that."

He covers my hand in his and he smiles. "Thank you for all you're doing, Beth. I'm so glad you're here."

My eyes scan his face but his smile doesn't reach his eyes. He's terrified. I give him a big hug and kiss his cheek. He leans into me.

We sit at the counter together and eat and chat about the day and how the new marketing plan is going. He seems to relax a little, acting less tense and scared as we talk about other things.

We finish eating and after we clean up the kitchen, we walk out back to sit with the dogs by the fire. I settle into the glider next to him and wrap a thick buffalo plaid blanket around us.

After dinner, Mellie and Kase join us for a while. I love watching Kase play with the puppies and seeing how happy they make him.

Mellie sits in a chair next to me and Evan tosses her a blanket to put over her lap.

"How's it going, Mellie? What are you reading?"

Mellie grins and holds up a Baker's Creek catalog. "Just dreaming about gardens and looking at seeds."

"That's actually not a bad idea."

"I liked helping with the small kitchen garden we had last summer. I didn't get the chance to plant anything because we got here after it was already going, but I think I'd like to restructure it. Maybe I can clean it out and plant some different things if you're okay with it, Evan."

"Yeah, that sounds great. Use the inn account when you order the seeds and we'll get everything else you need from the local garden store," Evan tells her. He explains the back story of the garden to me. "The Donegals, who used to live to the side of us, had a huge garden that we helped out with for many years. Now, they've both passed away and their grown kids are probably going to sell the property. I want to buy it and expand, but we just don't have the money for that. At least not yet."

"That would be amazing to expand. If we keep implementing our plans, hopefully we can get the money to make it happen," I say. The fact that I used the term "we" isn't lost on me, but I hurry to change the subject before Evan can catch on. "So what do you want to plant?" I ask Mellie.

She's now more excited than I've ever seen her. She goes on an absolute rant about heirloom tomatoes, beans, pumpkins, onions, and other various plants I'm not sure I'd know what to do with.

"I've always wanted to run a farmers' market back on the big lot in the back from March through October," Evan says.

Hearing them talk about all of these ideas for the future makes me sad I won't be here for it. I said sixty days, and time is going by too fast. I'm trying to ignore the fact that I want to see how the garden turns out and enjoy sharing whatever they grow with them. I want to help Mellie and watch it all unfold. It's safe to say that I am questioning my decision at this point.

I did say maybe...

"I would love to help organize that," she says.

"We'll definitely talk more about this," Evan says. "I love the idea."

Kase begins to yawn and curls up with the sleeping puppies. Mellie says, "That's our cue. Time to head out."

Evan stands and carries a sleepy Kase up the steps to the garden shed. Mellie looks at me and whispers loudly, "He's perfection. You know that?"

"I heard that..." Evan says.

I grin and shake my head. "Evan's great with him."

She has no idea how much this hits me. He's everything that I want but know I shouldn't have.

He comes back down a few minutes later and slides back into the glider beside me.

Mellie heads up to the loft and calls over her shoulder, "Have a good night, you two. Thanks, Evan."

I love my days and nights here with everyone. They make it easy for me to be me. Not the old me, but maybe the new me. I don't think I can ever go back to who I was before, but I'm starting to feel like this new version isn't so bad, either.

Evan and I snuggle and quietly watch the fire for a little bit until he whispers, "Ready to go inside?" into my ear.

We douse the fire then gather up the sleeping pups and

carry them into their kennel for the night. I get ready for bed in the bathroom while Evan does his nightly rounds.

I'm not sure where I should sleep so I lay on the bed in the guest room and read until he returns. I can't focus and basically just read the same page over and over. Finally, I hear him come in and his footsteps in the hall.

"This is where you want to sleep?" he asks as he leans against the frame of the door.

"I wasn't sure," I say.

I want to be with him. I want to curl up with him and sleep next to him, warm and cozy in his embrace. My brain is saying stay in this room, but my body and heart want to go with him to his room and never leave. All rational thought is pretty much gone at this point.

"You can sleep wherever you want to sleep," he says casually as he peels off his shirt slowly and stares at me. He has abs for days. Like too many to casually count. He leans against the doorway and stares at me seductively, his jeans hanging low and giving a nice view of the V muscle just above his groin. Then he casually turns and walks down the hall to his bedroom. This guy.

"Damn it," I swear as I hear him turn the shower on.

I turn the lamp off and pad down to his room. I slide under the covers on the side of the bed I slept in last night. To say I'm nervous is an understatement. Part of me wants to go back to the guest room. Staying in here means everything will change forever. It won't be me and John. Now it will really be me and Evan. That part of me will be gone forever, and that makes a part of me sad.

But I need Evan. He makes me feel more whole, something I haven't felt in six years. I want to really live my life. Just having him near me is so comforting.

When the shower stops, my heart pounds as he comes into the room. Water droplets bead across his bare chest and broad shoulders. All he wears is a revealing pair of boxer briefs and a towel around his neck. I have to force myself not to audibly gulp at the sight of him.

"That's better," he says as he balls up his towel and throws it in the hamper then slides under the covers next to me.

"What are you thinking about, Beth?" He opens his arms to welcome me into his embrace.

"It's been a while," I say quietly. "And I'm nervous."

"It's been a while for me, too. But I think we're good together." His large hands hold my face and he kisses me gently.

"This is going to change us," I whisper.

"I sure hope so. I like you, Beth. A lot."

I love him. I love how gentle yet protective he is with his family and guests. I love how he makes everyone feel safe and happy here. I want to tell him that, but I can't. I lamely said sixty days and maybe, and I can't tell him I love him or that I want to stay until I am absolutely certain that I do.

Moonlight streams in over the bed as he kisses me slowly. He lifts my t-shirt over my head and slides my sleep shorts down with his other hand while kissing me deeply. My arms wrap around him. I'm hungry for him. I want more, and I let him know by pressing myself against him.

He leans me back and kisses my neck all the way down my chest, pausing to caress and kiss me down my stomach as his hands move over my lower abdomen. I pray he doesn't see or feel my stretch marks. The evidence of who I was before. Mother to a precious baby who didn't make it. I don't mind my stretch marks; they remind me that she was real and she was here. I was her mom. I always will be.

It's my fault she didn't make it.

But he doesn't notice. Or if he does, he doesn't say anything. I know I'll have to tell him about her eventually, but not tonight. Tonight is ours. Tonight, my focus is Evan.

I kiss him back hungrily, and his pace meets mine. He moves between my legs and he finds me already wet.

"Beth," he says hoarsely.

"I need you," I say urgently.

"I need you, too," he says as he reaches toward his nightstand for a condom and grabs it with one hand as he pulls down his briefs.

I reach down and grab him, so turned on. Even more turned on now. He feels so good. I need him inside of me.

He pulls me across the bed, I feel weightless in his arms

as he reaches down to kiss me deeply.

He gently slides into me ever so slowly and I grip his back as my legs wrap around him and pull him deeper. He kisses me deeply, and he feels so good.

"You feel so good, Beth," he whispers, his breath hot against my ear.

"So do you," I moan as my body moves with his.

We move together, in perfect rhythm, and it doesn't matter that it's been a while for both of us, or that we were both nervous for this moment, it just feels *right*. The electric rush between the two of us at finally connecting after the pent-up tension is magic. He moves in and out of me, rolling onto his back to let me be in control. Before I know it, I'm tipping over the edge and stars are dotting my eyes. God, I needed him. He's been here all along, but now I can't imagine him not being mine.

I finally come and I tense all around him. He doesn't stop, flipping me back onto my back as he takes what he needs. His breaths become more jagged and it doesn't take long for him to come, too.

Afterward, we fall asleep, me wrapped in his warmth. Being with him is more amazing than I could have imagined, and at this moment, I know he's right. We *are* good together. My heart hurts to admit it, but maybe we could work. I just need to figure out how I can merge my life of pain with a life of hope.

CHAPTER 19

Beth

Maybe.

The sound of Evan's phone going off startles us awake. He sits up and answers, "Hello...?"

He pinches the bridge of his nose and sits up straighter, his legs swinging over the edge of the bed. I put my arms around him. I can hear Margie's voice on the other end of the line, and she sounds upset.

"Okay, I'm getting on the next flight. Keep me updated. Love you, Mom."

I squint at the clock. It's 2:38 am.

Evan hangs up and slides on jeans. He pulls a long-sleeved

t-shirt from his closet.

"What is it?" I ask, fearing the absolute worst.

"It's bad, Beth. He's been admitted to the hospital. We need to do the transplant as soon as I can get there." My heart breaks seeing him like this. I quickly think of what I can do to help.

I jump into action. "I'll take you to the airport."

Evan frantically packs his bag and gets ready. The dogs whimper in their kennel and he heads to the kitchen to tend to them.

"Making us coffees to-go, then I'm ready," he calls from the kitchen.

I quickly dash out to the guest room where all my stuff is to get dressed in leggings and a sweatshirt. I pull my hair up, brush my teeth, and slide on my Converse.

I head to the kitchen where I wrap my arms around him and hug him close. He hugs me back and says, "Ready?"

"Yes." I pour coffee into two travel mugs and we head out to his truck. He looks nervous and worried. I don't know what to say so I just slide my hand over his.

"Thank you for being here. I can't even tell you how much I appreciate you right now. You have been doing so much for me and my family."

"Hey, I will be here and help in any way you need me to while you are gone. Just take care of yourself and do what you need to do for Caleb. Focus on your family."

We pull up to the airport and I give him a quick kiss goodbye. He hugs me tight and kisses me for a long time. He looks at me, full of worry. "I'm falling in love with you, Beth."

I kiss him again, deeper. I am too, but I can't tell him. I can't get his hopes up. I don't know what's going to happen yet, and I won't make promises that I can't keep.

Instead, I just look in his eyes and say, "Maybe I am, too."

That seems to put him at ease. "Maybe."

"Safe travels. Hug everyone for me."

"Bye, Beth," he says as he walks into the airport, his duffle over his shoulder.

When I get back to the inn, it's already after 4 a.m. I check on the dogs and start getting ready for the day. I can't sleep and the best way for me not to worry is to stay busy. I head over to the front room, start a fire in the fireplace, and get the coffee bar set up for the day.

I pour myself a cup and go over our bookings and schedule. Everything looks great and I'm so excited. I feel like I have a purpose here and I'm helping. It feels really good to feel needed again.

Just after 6 a.m, Mellie comes in. I pour her a cup of coffee and we sit on the couch together.

"Why are you up so early?" she asks me.

"Caleb was admitted and they need to do his transplant as soon as Evan can get there."

Mellie's face falls and worry shrouds her face. "Where is he?"

"I took him to the airport a few hours ago. He took a flight first thing this morning."

"Wow. I can't even imagine. This is so scary," she says.

"He promised to give us an update as soon as he has one."

"Okay, so I guess now we wait," she says.

"That's all we can do," I agree.

Now the corners of her mouth curl up in a sly smile. "How was your first night at his place?" she asks.

"It was good."

"It was *good*?" She raises one eyebrow at me.

"Okay, fine, it was *great*," I relent. "But then we got the call about Caleb and now I'm just so sad and worried."

I don't want to tell her too much. I'm still not sure what Evan and I are doing. I still have a lot of processing to do with all this new information. And he's still her boss. I don't want to make it weird.

Luckily, she changes the subject. "I hope Caleb's okay," she says, looking concerned. "He's practically the same age as Kase. I can't even imagine what Allie is going through. She must be worried sick."

I don't tell her that I can well imagine what Allie's going through. Instead, I say, "I know. There's not much we can do to help with Caleb, but we can work hard on the fall festival to make more money for the inn. Has Evan talked to you about the loan situation?"

"Not really, though I know we need that festival to bring in money, and I know Sasha's been cutting back. How can I help?"

"I'm so glad you asked." I grin at her as I flip open my notebook.

"I think we need to do things up big. Like before, when Mr. Harper was running it."

"I love it. I haven't ever planned anything like this, but I'll do my best to help any way I can."

"You'll do great. I have it planned for October 14th and 15th. Pete is checking our insurance policy and making sure that it is still up to date with all of this. I have a signup list for vendors and volunteers in the community. And I made signs."

"How can I help?"

"Can you distribute the signs in town? I may also need help nailing down a few of the games, vendors, and donations for prizes."

"I can do that."

"We're doing a corn maze, a pumpkin patch with a local farmer, inflatables, and a paintball gallery."

"Oh, wow. This is going to be so fun."

"Yeah, and the best part..." I lean in. "Don't tell Sasha,

but Pete made a pumpkin cannon, and he wants to surprise her with it."

"Okay, he does not want to surprise her with that. He wants to quietly create it in the hope she won't say no." She laughs.

"Exactly." Watching the way Pete and Sasha razz each other but seeing how much they love each other at the same time has been fun. They're definitely couple goals.

"The best part is that the Bullock farm is going to do an airplane candy drop both days at 3 p.m for the kids."

"Kase will love that. I mean, he'll love all of it, but that's going to be awesome for the kids."

"Right? And some of the local bands will fill time slots to have live music playing. It's going to be such a great time."

"How many people do you think will come?"

"I don't know, but I have a feeling it's going to be amazing."

"It will be."

I go over the rest of my to-dos with Mellie, who takes on a few more things from my list to help out with. By the time we're done, we can smell breakfast back in the kitchen and our stomachs are grumbling.

Mellie heads over to wake up Kase and get ready for the day and I already feel so energized, despite my lack of sleep. I feel like the plan is really coming together to save the inn. This is one way I feel like I can help Evan and his family. I finally feel like I have a purpose again and it feels so good.

I can't stop thinking about Evan and I text him.

> **Beth**: Hey, did you make it okay? I already miss you.
>
> **Evan**: Yes, headed to my connecting flight. I miss you too. How are things going?
>
> **Beth**: All is well. Mellie and I are working on the fall festival prep. Pete is getting outside things ready, and Sasha is ordering the food we'll need. Everything is great here, no need to worry. Puppies miss you.
>
> **Evan**: I really can't thank you enough.

My mind races back to last night and I can think of several ways he can thank me. Of course, I know this is not the time, so I bring the focus back to his family.

> **Beth**: Give everyone a big hug for me when you see them. We're all sending our love and healing thoughts.

For the next several days, I settle into a satisfying routine with the dogs, Mellie, Kase, Pete, and Sasha. We all eat together, work together, and spend time together to plan the festival. It doesn't seem like work. Every single minute is fun, and I feel so at ease with these people—like they could really be *my* people.

One night, after I tuck the pups into their kennel for bed,

I make the rounds to shut everything down. That's when I run into Pete, who's apparently doing the same. "Hey, Beth, what are you doing out so late?"

"Night rounds, like Evan showed me."

"You don't have to do that, but we appreciate you so much for helping."

"Aw, thanks, Pete. How are things coming along on your list for the festival?"

"Good. I have a tractor ready for hayrides, and one of the neighboring farms is dropping off bales of hay tomorrow."

Before Pete can continue, we're distracted by some motion at the front porch. We see a person stick something to the front door then race away.

I head over to investigate and find a bright yellow paper taped to the front door as the person drives off in an Audi. I snatch the paper down.

Warning:
Foreclosure Notice

Pete exclaims, "What the hell?"

"Who was that?" I ask.

"Hamilton McGraw, the bank manager. He's trying to screw with us. We're not in foreclosure. He's trying to hurt our business by messing with guests. He probably posted it now, thinking we wouldn't see it until tomorrow and hoped some of our guests would see it first."

"Evan said he had until January."

"You know about that?" Pete asks, surprised.

"Yes, that's why we've been developing this plan to amp up the bookings. It's working. We're now booked through the end of the year. As far as I can tell, we're doing well. Other than the festival, I'm not sure what else we could be doing."

"Me neither," Pete says. "But I don't know if we should tell Evan right now. I think it will just upset him and he has other things to focus on."

"I actually have an idea. I know a lawyer through my friend Logan I can reach out to. Let me see if he can do anything. This is harassment, and there has to be a way to put an end to it."

Pete looks at me with a combination of skepticism and hope. "Okay. Anything you can do to help is good. But still, let's wait to tell Evan until he comes back."

CHAPTER 20

I never told you
about this...

I wake up groggy and look around, still feeling woozy. "How's Caleb?" I ask my mom, who's sitting in the chair next to my bed, reading a book.

"He's doing great, honey. You did so good, too. I'm so proud of you both." She reaches over to pat my hand.

I nod and doze off again, glad to know the little guy is okay. I dream of Beth and wake up again when the nurse comes in to take my vitals.

"Mr. Harper, do you need help using the restroom? I can

help you get up and moving."

I nod and try to sit up in the bed. I'm stiff and somewhat sore.

I walk for a bit around my hospital room and stretch my legs. Surprisingly, I'm not in as much pain as I thought I would be. I'm just really tired.

I feel too nauseous to eat so I lie down to try and go back to sleep again, but I'm anxious to check on Caleb, who's on another floor. I need to get stronger to walk there. I know my mom said he's doing okay, but I can't relax until I see for myself.

I nod off for a while. When I wake up again, Allie is standing over my bed. "Hi," I whisper groggily. "How's he doing?"

"He's doing really well. Thank you, Evan." She leans down and kisses me on the cheek.

"Give him a hug for me. I'll be in to see him when I can."

"Just get some rest and let me know what I can do to help you."

"Can you ask the nurse for some food? I'm so hungry."

"Will do." She heads out into the hall.

I pick my phone from the hospital tray table and scan my messages. Lots of well wishes from everyone back home and no bad news from Hamilton.

When I'm finally able to stand steadily, I slip on my shoes and pad down the hall to the nurses' station to ask if I can take a shower. Three nurses' heads swivel to me in interest. One of them clears her throat and says, "Mr. Harper, do you need help with your shower?" One of the nurses snickers and turns her head.

I laugh nervously. "I think I'll be fine. I just wanted to check and see if it was okay."

The only woman I want to help me shower right now is Beth. I miss her, and I hate that I had to leave after our first night together. When we first met, I had no idea how much she would come to mean to me. I had a feeling on my end, but I didn't know if she would ever let me in. Now I can't imagine my life without her. Going through this big surgery has made me realize even more just how precious life is and not to take a single minute of it for granted. I can't wait to get back to her and soak up our time together, especially if she decides not to stay.

Shaking my head to clear that thought, I shuffle down the hall back to my room, trying to hold the back of my hospital gown together, I hear the nurses burst out laughing.

"He's so freaking gorgeous," one of them mumbles.

Another one says, "Those green eyes…"

Someone whispers, "That beard…"

I just keep walking. Jesus. I have to get out of here and home to Beth.

I shower and feel a million times better as I step out and carefully dry the area around my incision. I get dressed and dial a video call to Beth.

"How are you feeling?" she asks, speaking softly.

"Not too bad," I tell her. "Why are you talking so quietly?"

"Kase is here, napping on the couch."

"Aw, how are things going over there?"

"Evan, I am so excited about the fall festival. It looks like we're able to bring back some of your dad's traditions, plus we've brought in some fun new ones that I can't wait for you to see."

"Like what?" I lean back and get comfortable. I love hearing her talk so excitedly about the inn. Given how excited everyone is for the festival, we need to make this a permanent future tradition again. I just hope we can save the inn to be able to do that.

"Okay, you can't tell Sasha, but Pete is making a pumpkin cannon to surprise her."

"You know she's not going to like that, right?" I laugh.

"That's exactly what Mellie said, too." She laughs. "But it will definitely be fun to watch it play out."

I think back to the time a few years ago he tried to surprise her with a pumpkin trebuchet and he accidentally knocked over her pie table. Sasha was not pleased.

"We have a whole sheet of volunteers and I've planned everything down to the tiniest details."

"That all sounds really great, Beth. Everyone is going to love this."

"I hope so," she says.

"I miss you. Can't wait to get cleared to come home to you."

"We all miss you."

"What do you mean '*we*' all? Don't you miss me, Beth?" I tease.

"Yes," she says quietly and I see her try to hide her smile.

"How much?"

"Well, when you get home, I'll show you."

I take a deep breath and wince a little. I'm still stiff and uncomfortable from my surgery. "I'll hold you to that."

"I'm so glad you called. I didn't want to bother you, but I've done nothing but think about you guys nonstop. When do they think you'll be able to fly home?"

"Probably in a few days."

"Is that... too soon?"

"No, I'm good."

"What about your wounds?"

I laugh a little. "Beth, I'm a combat medic. I'm good with basic wound care."

"I guess you're right. Well, then come home. I'll be your nurse."

"You know, the nurses here all volunteered to help me shower..."

"Which nurses? They're all dead," she says.

I laugh. "I showered alone. You're the only woman I want

in the shower with me."

"There's a lot of things I want to do with you. It's weird not being with you."

"Are you rethinking the sixty days idea and planning a permanent residency?"

"Maybe. I don't know. A lot is happening. I feel like we don't have to decide anything today. Just live in the moment. And for the moment, I like helping you with the inn and being around your family."

I breathe a sigh of relief. Hopefully she gives up this whole "leaving" nonsense. It's clear she belongs here. We haven't known each other long, but sometimes when you know, you know...

"How's Caleb?"

"I'm going to check on him as soon as the nurse clears me to go to the pediatric floor. I tried to go earlier, but I was too nauseous. I can't wait to see him. He's apparently taking the kidney well and already doing so much better. Everything has gone well so far."

"I am so glad to hear that. I can't wait to tell everyone else. We've all been praying and sending healing thoughts your way. Your mom's been really good about giving us updates, but I can't help but worry."

"It'll be okay. What else's new?" She's quiet for a minute and looks away. I can tell something's up. "What?"

"Well, I didn't want to tell you until after your surgery

because I didn't want you to worry, but Hamilton slapped a premature foreclosure notice on the door late one night. Pete and I actually saw him do it so we took it down before any guests were able to see it, but it was still a shitty thing to do. I reached out to a lawyer I know through Logan and asked him what he thought we could do, and he said we can file a complaint with the bank, maybe even threaten a lawsuit."

My breath hitches and I take a deep breath and scratch my chin. I haven't met this friend Logan yet, and I'm hesitant to share our troubles with an outsider. But if Beth trusts him, I know I can trust him, too. "Okay, thanks for letting me know. Just keep an eye out for that guy. We have new accounts set up that are not with his bank so he can't poke his nose around in our business anymore."

I'm pissed Hamilton is doing this when he probably knows I am gone and thinks he can get away with it.

"I'm sorry. I wanted to wait to tell you, but it felt like you really needed to know."

"No, it's fine. I'm glad you told me, Beth."

"Pete's looking out, too."

I'm relieved to hear that Pete is on top of things, too. I hate being so far away and being unable to look out for my inn.

"Let me know if you need me to do anything before you come. I'll pick you up. Send me your flight information."

The nurse comes in to take my vitals. "I have to go now. Thanks for holding down the fort."

"Bye," she says softly, her kind eyes not leaving mine until we hang up.

When the nurse leaves, my mom comes in and I decide it's time to tell her about Hamilton. I can tell by the look on her face that she has something to say.

"What?"

She takes a deep breath before she speaks. "I never told you this, but I think Hamilton is mad about something to do with me."

"What do you mean?"

"Before I met your dad, Hamilton wanted to date me, and I turned him down. I always thought he was resentful about that, and things always seemed a bit tense with him, but I generally try to steer clear of him and the bank. Your dad handled most of that stuff. But I wonder if now, even after all these years, he could be taking my rejection of him out on the inn."

My thoughts roll back a couple of weeks when he asked if my mom would be coming with me to the meeting at the bank. Things are starting to make sense now. He has a thing for my freaking mom and he's screwing with our inn because of it. What an asshole.

"Thank you for telling me, Mom. We're going to be free from him soon. We're going to pay the loan he's holding over us and that will be that. He won't get away with messing around with us like this anymore."

My mom just nods and then walks with me down to Caleb's room. My breath tightens a little when I see his tiny body in his hospital bed, my sister sitting at his side.

He's watching *PJ Masks* on TV and turns to greet me as I walk in. "Uncle Evan!" His little arms reach out for me and I lean in and give him a careful hug. "Hey, kidney bean twin, how are you?"

My mom looks so happy. Every time all of us are together, it makes me really wish Allie lived closer.

"What are you thinking?" Allie asks.

"That despite the circumstances, it's good for all of us to be together."

"I can't wait to move home to New Hampshire," Allie tells me. "When he's cleared for travel, I think I want to move back. I am so ready."

"Will your job let you work remotely?"

"We have been remote, but I still have to help with big events sometimes and go into the city. I've asked repeatedly to be able to be fully remote, but they don't want me to leave the state of California and be so far away that I can't go into the city as needed."

"We could definitely use your help around the inn if you moved back."

"I would love that. I can't wait to be home. Speaking of

the inn, Mom told me what Hamilton did. What a sleazeball. How dare he?"

"What's a sleazeball, Momma?" Caleb asks.

"A bad guy, honey." She quickly changes the subject. "I hear the nurses have a thing for you," Allie teases me, making a pretend throwing up gesture. "They're all asking about you. If you're single or not. What should I tell them?" she asks with a smirk.

"Taken," I say, returning her smirk.

"Oh, really," she says, shocked.

"I'm seeing Beth. I think it's serious." It feels good to say it out loud. She means so much to me and I want my family to know about us.

"She still talking about leaving?" my mom asks worriedly.

"We're still working on that. But we really like each other and I'm making sure she knows how much I want her to stay. How much I can't imagine not having her with us."

"I like Beth a lot," my mom comments, leaning back in her chair.

"I'm happy for you, Evan. It's about time," my sister says.

I roll my eyes but smile at Allie. She gets on my nerves, as sisters do, but I'm so thankful for her. At the end of the day, family is all we have. I'm just glad they're all okay.

CHAPTER 21

Beth

Busted

A delivery arrives, I believe for the fall festival, and I meet the truck around back. When I open the barn door to unload the truck, I can't believe what I see inside.

"What in the hell?" I say out loud when I discover my car parked in there. I find Pete cleaning out the fire pits. My hands firmly on my hips, I ask him point blank, "How long has my car been in that barn?"

He gives me a deer in the headlights look, then shakes his head and wanders off.

Fuming, I open my phone and take a picture of my car. I

text the image to Evan.

Beth: BUSTED.

He calls me immediately, but when he answers with a simple, "Hey," I can't be mad at him. Just hearing his voice puts me at ease and makes me miss him more. But he doesn't need to know that now. Not right away.

"How long has my car been in the barn? And how much do I owe for the repairs? I need answers!"

"It's okay. I traded singing gigs for your car repairs. Sam finished working on it and put it there just before I left. I knew you could drive my truck while I was gone, and I didn't want to tell you because I didn't want you to worry about the cost or paying me back."

"What am I going to do with you?"

"I can think of some things," he flirts.

"I miss you," I add quietly.

"I know, beautiful. I'm coming home tomorrow. Did you get my flight information? I can't wait to see you."

"Yes, I'll be there. I can't wait for you to see everything we've done so far for the festival. It's going to be amazing."

"You're amazing," he says.

"I may be just a little amazing," I shoot back playfully but with a sense of confidence I haven't felt in so long.

"I can't wait to show you how grateful I am." God, I hope Margie isn't around to hear any of this.

"Okay, well you still need to rest. I'll play nurse for you." I try to be serious but a laugh escapes.

He laughs back until his tone gets serious. "So Allie says she's going to try to move back now that Caleb has had his surgery. I can't wait for you to meet them... I mean, if you stay," he adds.

I avoid replying directly because I'm not sure how to answer right now, so instead I say, "That will be great for you to have them closer."

"We have a lot to still talk about when I get home," he says quietly.

I change the subject because I know where he's going with this.

"Did you hear anything about Hamilton? Logan's coming for the weekend and he's bringing his friend Preston, the lawyer. I wanted to talk to him more about all of this. Are you okay with that?"

"Of course. I trust you. Let me know what he says. Also, I have some new information about Hamilton, but I'll share all that with you tomorrow when I see you."

"Okay, Ev. I can't wait to see you tomorrow."

"Me, too. Bye for now."

When Logan and Preston arrive, I give Logan a hug and

shake Preston's hand. "I'm so happy you both came. Come in," I say, relieved to have them here.

Logan smiles at me. "You look good, Beth. Happy." He sets his bag down by the front desk. He doesn't look happy.

"It's nice to finally meet you, Preston."

Preston smiles at me. "Nice to meet you, Beth. Don't mind old grouchy here. He just found out his lady has become 'exclusive' with someone else and he's a little cranky. He needs this getaway, bad."

"Oh, no," I say, looking at Logan. "What happened to Jennifer?"

"It was Jessica. And she wanted to be serious and I didn't, so she found someone else to be serious with." He shakes his head and looks away. I can tell he's upset but trying to save face in front of Preston, so I make a mental note to ask him more about it later. For now, I play along.

I stare at Logan, trying to figure out what to say. "Were you not ready to be serious with her? I thought you had been together for a while."

"We had fun. But I'm just not the settling down type," he says.

He's definitely a bit of a playboy, and I've never known him to be serious with any woman. He comes from money, yet he is a total workaholic and doesn't have time for much. We get along well because we both work a lot and have the publishing world in common, but he's still one of my best friends and I'm worried for him. I lean in and give him a hug, his arms reaching around to hug me back.

"What's this for?" he says.

"I've missed you."

"Missed you, too. Can't wait for the tour of this place. It looks incredible."

I get them both checked into their rooms and hand them their keys, then they each head to their rooms to get situated before dinner. Sasha's been cooking up a storm and the aromas have been teasing me all day.

Before dinner, I head over to the cottage to grab the dogs and bring them to the inn for the evening. The guests generally enjoy playing with them, and of course, so does Kase.

"Come on, babies. Let's go." I hook their leashes, which they're still trying to get used to. I have become attached to both of them and I have a feeling Evan might be a teensy bit upset when he comes home and finds out they've been sleeping with me in his bed. They are also the snuggliest dogs ever.

I put the puppies in their pen then head into the dining room. Preston and Logan are already sitting with everyone, and appear to be fitting right in.

Mellie comes over to me and whispers, "Who is that guy?"

"Which one?" I ask.

I look over at both of them laughing and making jokes

with another guest. "Logan is the one with the brown hair, goatee, and blue sweater. He's my literary agent and best friend. Next to him is his friend Preston, the blonde haired one with the blue eyes, who is an attorney and has come with Logan to help give some advice for the inn."

"Preston's cute. I mean, they're both really cute, to be honest. Are all of your friends cute?" she asks with a laugh.

"Do you want me to hook you up?" I ask with a sly smile.

"No, that's okay. I'm good. I was just curious."

"Are you sure? Preston is a rich attorney," I tease.

Something in Mellie's face changes and her energy shifts. I can't read her expression, but she looks bothered in some way. I make a note to ask her about it later.

Mellie makes plates for her and Kase then carries them off to a side table. I don't miss the way she looks at Preston as she passes him. I also don't miss the way he watches her when she's not looking.

I make a plate of chicken and dumplings and join my friends.

"So? What do you think?" I ask them.

"We can definitely see why you love it here," Preston says, taking another quick glance at Mellie. He gets up and grabs his plate for seconds. "The food is incredible."

Sasha is standing in ear shot and I know she's heard him because she nods at me approvingly. I give her a thumbs up.

"It definitely has amazing perks," I say as I take a bite. I moan with pleasure. "So good."

"Is there somewhere quiet we can talk business later?" Logan asks.

"Evan has a cottage in the back we can use. I've been staying there."

Logan raises his eyebrows at me with this admission.

"What?" I say, staring right back at him.

"As your best friend and stand-in protective older brother, if you had one, I'm just looking out for you. Are you a couple now? Should we call you Be-Evan?"

Preston and Logan laugh, and I roll my eyes. "He comes home tomorrow. I dare you both to say that to his face."

Logan shakes his head. "Nope, not messing with that guy. You said he's a former Marine. He could probably kill me with his bare hands. I'm just a book nerd."

"Yeah, like you couldn't defend yourself." I smirk as I take a sip of my water.

"I won't piss off the man who holds my best friend's heart in his hands," Logan says. "You look really happy right now. This place has been good for you."

"I know. I am very happy. I just…"

"Just what?" he asks. My best friend knows me well, and I know him well enough to know he knows something's up and he's not going to let it rest. But now's not the time.

I shake my head. "We can talk about it later."

We finish eating and help clean up. I watch Sasha and Pete

head up the hill to their cottage for the night and I get a pang in my heart.

I *do* want what they have. I want a forever with someone. But with everything that has happened to me in my life… I know that forever doesn't exist. At least not for me.

I want to be with Evan, but when you lose someone who means so much to you, it breaks you in ways that you can never put yourself back together again. It's hard to love again and risk that pain. Irrational, maybe, but it's what I am dealing with.

I leash up Bossy and Chip and take them to the fire pits where Mellie and Kase are sitting along with a few other guests. Kase immediately comes to play with the puppies and I settle in next to Mellie.

Mellie looks over and says, "Evan texted. I think he's bored. I'm helping with the puppies while you go get him tomorrow."

"Thanks. It feels like it's been forever."

"Beth, when he comes home…" she trails off and looks away. Then she turns back to face me. "Are you really leaving like you said? He is going to be devastated."

What do I say? I stare into the fire pit, looking for answers. I'm scared. We've worked hard to turn things around, but is it enough?

A lump forms in my throat. I'm a nomad, but this is their home. Their livelihood. What if they lose it? I could have done better.

I shake off my anxiety and turn my attention back to Mellie.

"You think we're going to make it?" I ask her.

"The inn or you and Evan?"

"Both," I whisper.

She looks me in the eye and says fiercely, "Yes, to both. We won't settle for any less."

Preston and Logan join us at the fire, and Preston offers," "Ready for that chat?"

I nod and stand, my mind still on what Mellie said. But now I have more pressing things to discuss with them.

"I'll bring you the puppies later, if that's okay?" Mellie asks. I watch Kase who is playing tug-of-war with Bossy and her rope toy.

"Sure," I say with a gentle squeeze on her arm.

We head inside and settle onto the sectional where I give them all the details of the situation I know from Evan. Preston takes notes as I speak and asks me some questions I can't answer, but both the guys are aghast at what I'm telling them.

"What an asshole," Logan says, and I emphatically agree. "Can he keep getting away with doing this?" he asks Preston directly.

Preston shakes his head. "Sounds like the classic bully—all bluster and likely less powerful than he thinks. Let me do some investigating. And when Evan gets back," now he addresses me, "I'm going to need to talk to him. When he's feeling up to it."

"Thank you. I know Margie and Evan will really appreciate it," I tell him.

"No one deserves to be treated this way," Logan adds.

Something occurs to me. "You know, Freedom Valley is a really supportive community. I wonder if he's doing this to other businesses as well, and if anyone else would be willing to join us in fighting back."

"Either way, hopefully we can send a message so this stops here," Preston adds. "This does seem like a really nice town. It would be terrible for one guy to wreck the whole vibe."

"Have you been here before?"

"Not for years. My family and I used to visit the area in the fall to see the foliage. It's a pretty quick drive from Boston. Seeing it again, I still really love it here. I'm actually considering maybe getting a weekend place or something."

"It's definitely a great little town," I tell him. And from what I've seen of it, I know I'm not just saying that. The tavern, the coffee shop, with all of the nice people who work in those places. The beautiful quiet vistas where Evan has taken me. It would be a nice place to call home.

Preston interrupts my musings with a pointed question about Mellie. "So that blonde you were talking to out there. What's her story?"

"Funny you should ask," I tease.

"What?" he wonders.

"She asked about you, as well," I say with a smile.

Logan grins. "You just gave me crap about my love life. Maybe it's time you find someone, Preston, so I can give you crap about yours."

"Who's in love?" Preston deflects. "I was just curious about her. I mean, you'd have to be blind not to see how pretty she is. But..." he hesitates.

"But what?" I press, feeling protective of Mellie.

"She seems, well, a little jumpy? I feel like maybe there's something off there?"

"She's really great," I assure him. "She may be a little jumpy, but she has her story, like we all do. Who knows? Stick around and give her a chance, and maybe someday she'll share it with you?"

I glance over at Logan, who's wearing a shit-eating grin. I continue, "Hey, maybe you both should stick around, and we'll find you some nice women here in Freedom Valley to settle down with. We can host our very own version of The Bachelor," I say, then bust out laughing.

Logan cocks an eyebrow at me. "So you're staying here in Freedom Valley," he chides.

I immediately stop laughing. "I didn't say that," I tell him.

Logan chuckles. "You're my best friend, Beth, and I know you well. You didn't have to say it, and I still know it."

I start to feel a little cornered and I cut him off with a quick, "Agree to disagree."

He sighs, pretending we're going to sweep this under the rug but we both know he's going to press about it again. Instead of doing that now, however, he deflects and tells me, "I'm good with no relationship right now, thanks. Or ever. I just want to focus on my career. I'm up for a big promotion, and I need to stay focused," he says. "But Preston here…"

Preston is scribbling into his notebook. He seems to have lost interest in our conversation long ago.

"Preston?" I ask.

He looks up, in a daze. "Say what?"

Logan switches gears again. "I was waiting to talk to you about—"

I cut him off. "I don't want to talk about Evan and my staying here in Freedom Valley right now. Possibly ever."

He shakes his head. "If you would let me finish, I would tell you that I have news about *Let it Rain*."

"What about it?" I ask, a lump forming in my throat. My first book. I'm prepared to hear about some bad reviews or something of that nature when Logan surprises me.

"Someone wants to buy the rights for the film. And Montage wants to talk about a two-book deal. This is happening, Beth."

If I let it…

I take a deep breath. "What's the advance?"

"It's big, still negotiating. Could set you up for a while. You could just settle in here and write."

"What's the catch?"

"No more hermit status. You have to build your social media and agree to speaking engagements. Otherwise, it's never going to happen."

I bite my lip. So much has changed in the weeks I've been here. Even since the last time Logan made it clear what would be expected of me, really. It's amazing, but somehow I feel less ambivalent, instead I feel more strong and secure. Like I've finally made progress toward healing and being ready for something new. Something has definitely changed in me because I barely fight my residual anxiety at all as the word falls out of my mouth.

"Okay."

Logan sits up straighter. "Okay? Really?" He looks at me, scanning my face. "That's it? Just like that, you're agreeing to it?"

I nod. "Yeah. Let's do it."

CHAPTER 22

I love you.

My plane touches down. I hurry to baggage claim, grab my bag, and make my way to the curb outside arrivals. I'm not there two minutes before Beth pulls up in my truck. She jumps out and runs to me, hugging me tight. God, she smells so good. I cling to her and I never want to let go.

"I missed you," I murmur into her ear, pulling her closer.

"I missed you more."

As she drives us back to the inn, she catches me up with all the details about the fall festival and her conversation with the lawyer. She's so excited about everything, I can't imagine she still wants to leave us anymore.

"Are you paying attention?" she asks. "I can't wait for you to meet Logan and Preston. I told them everything I know, and Preston has some ideas. Of course he needs to speak with you directly, if you're feeling up to it."

"Of course, and thanks for doing that. We'll take all the help we can get." As usual, I'm overwhelmed about the finances. Now that Caleb is doing better, I can focus fully on the inn.

"Are you worried you won't have the money in time?" she asks.

"No, I think it's going okay. I just worry I'll mess something up. I shouldn't have gotten to this point in the first place. I should have come up with all the things you suggested on my own. I should have worked harder."

She knits her eyebrows. "You've been doing the best you can. Everyone is proud of you, and we all missed you so much."

"Maybe…" I can't help but feel like she's exaggerating a little.

"Everything is good at home, Ev. Seriously. Just focus on healing." I don't say anything and she glances over at me, looking worried.

I grin at her.

"What?"

"You said *home*."

She grins back. "I did."

"So does this mean you think of The Golden Gable as home, too?"

"Maybe..." she says.

I decide to stop pressing and just enjoy spending time with her while we're still alone. "Missed you," I say, raising her hand in mine and kissing her wrist.

"The puppies missed you the most."

"Oh. Chip and Bossy missed me the most? Really?" I smirk at her.

"Yes," she lies and grins.

"We'll see about that."

Beth and I are snuggling on the couch watching Netflix and I can tell something's bothering her. She rests her head on my shoulder, puppies curled into us and snoring peacefully. I wonder what she's thinking about; I know what I'm thinking.

We're like a family.

I love this. I love us. I want these nights on the couch on cold nights. Family dinners. Snuggles. Puppies. Future kids. I want this. Bad. Doesn't she?

I have to know what's up. "Hey, are you okay? Did I do something wrong?"

"What?" she asks absently, a faraway look in her eyes.

"No, I'm just really glad you're home. I've just been thinking about the inn. I'm worried you could lose it and what that could mean for everyone here."

"I know. I think about it, too, all the time. Believe me. But no matter what happens, know how grateful we all are for all you've done. The best thing to ever happen to me is to find you on the highway that day."

She kisses me deeply. She pulls back a little and I can't help but tell her how I feel. "I love you. I just want you to know that. You don't have to say anything back; I just wanted you to know."

She looks scared. "But what if I *can't* love you back?" she says and starts to cry. When I try to comfort her, she pushes me aside and heads out the door.

"Beth." I take a deep breath. I grab my coat and chase after her.

There are two men sitting at the firepits. When I pass, the one wearing a white hoodie stands and walks toward me. "Hey, are you Evan?"

"I am."

"I'm Logan," he says. I reach out and shake his outstretched hand. Beth didn't mention Logan was our age and not bad on the eyes. When she mentioned a literary agent, I pictured an older man in a sweater vest. Now I have questions.

"This is Preston," he says, nodding to the other guy, who's

now standing next to Logan, his hands tucked into the front of his jeans.

"Hey, man, thanks for coming," I tell him. "Beth told me you had some insights about the inn."

Preston reaches out and shakes my hand as well. "It's no problem. You have a great place here, and I know Beth is determined to help you find a way to hold on to it."

I shake his hand. "I appreciate any advice you can offer."

While I'd like to discuss some of Preston's ideas with him, now's not the time. I have to find Beth. I'm worried about how upset she got when I told her I loved her. "Speaking of Beth, have you seen her?"

"She tore through here a few minutes ago," Logan says. "She was heading that way." He points to the garden shed. The lights are on, so I assume she's up there talking to Mellie.

"What happened?" Preston asks.

"I think I may have messed things up."

"How?" Logans eyes narrow, and now their relationship becomes evident to me. This is just the kind of look I would give any dude who said he messed things up with my sister. Logan is like a brother to her.

I relax a bit and confess, "I told her I loved her and then she took off."

Logan's mouth goes into a firm line. "Ah, yeah, I get it. Look, Beth's been through some things. She just needs a little time to sort things out. She'll come around, I'm sure of it. Just be patient."

CHAPTER 23

Beth

We are stronger
than you think.

I race over to Mellie's. She's musing over a seed catalog with a mug of tea as I barge in on her.

"Can I come in?" I glance around, not seeing Kase and realizing he's probably already asleep.

"Of course. Would you like some tea?"

"Sure. Thanks," I say, trying to push the feelings of panic away.

Mellie pours a mug in her kitchenette and brings it to me. We sit on her living room rug for a few minutes, sipping at our steaming mugs, before Mellie gently asks, "Do you want to talk about it?"

I love how Mellie doesn't push. She can sit quietly with you, and you just know that she's there for you. You don't feel alone.

"I'm not really sure," I tell her. "I have a hard time letting people in. Honestly, I would never want anyone to carry what I've been carrying. It's just too awful."

Mellie shifts her legs under her. "But isn't that what friends and family are for? To carry you when you need to be carried? And you do the same for them?"

"How did you get so wise?" It's hard to imagine I wasn't much older than Mellie is now when I lost everything in the blink of an eye.

"People tell me I'm an old soul." She smiles, but her smile doesn't reach her eyes. There's pain there, too.

"But that's not really it," she tells me. "I carry my own trauma. And you know who also carries it with me? Evan. He's the only one who knows the truth about where Kase and I are from, and he's kept our secret. People are stronger than you think, Beth. It's not fair to judge other people's strengths or what other people can handle or not."

"He told me he loves me."

"And what did you say?" she hedges.

"I told him I'm not sure I can love him back."

"But it seems like you *do* love him," she says.

I nod and a tear slides down my cheek as I take another sip of my tea. We hear someone coming up the stairs quietly and Mellie stiffens and relaxes when we hear Evan's deep voice. "It's just me. I'm looking for Beth."

Mellie leans in and whispers. "I think things are going to be okay, Beth. Let him in. Tell him."

I nod and set my tea down.

Evan comes into the living room and I stand to greet him. He leans over me and kisses my cheek before pulling me in for a hug. I lean into him and my eyes fill with tears.

Mellie takes our mugs to the kitchen. "I think you have a lot to talk about," she tells us.

I thank Mellie with a quick hug, then Evan and I quietly tiptoe down the stairs so we don't wake Kase. We head to the firepit area, where no one else is around. He stokes a fire and we sit in a swinging chair together.

"I know I need to tell you more of my story, but I don't even know where to begin…" I take a deep breath. I know it's time to tell him, but am I ready for him to know everything?

"My mom died when I was six. I never knew my dad. We were poor, and she never went to the doctor for herself. It was like she was so busy taking care of me that she didn't take care of herself. I felt like if she had taken care of herself more instead of only worrying about me, maybe they would have caught the cancer earlier and she wouldn't have died."

"Oh, Beth, I'm so sorry." He pulls me close to him.

"She didn't have a plan for me, and I ended up in foster care, always bouncing around various homes. I was the smelly kid at school who didn't have money to wash my clothes, or even shower sometimes."

My chest burns with the memory of an early morning in the bathroom at school. "One morning at school, I was trying to wash my clothes in the sink when this girl comes in and tells me she has something for me. I was skeptical, because most kids just bullied me, but she handed me a Target bag with clothes, underwear, and socks. All clean."

"That was Cara?" he asks.

I nod. "That one act of kindness changed my life. She became my best friend that day. She protected me from bullies and invited me to her house often. Her parents were always so kind to me. When I aged out of the system when I was eighteen, Cara's family took me in. That's when I finally got to feel what it was like to have stability in my life. I got to live with my best friend, I had food every day, clean clothes to wear, and I got to finish high school.

"Cara's family taught me what having a family was truly like, what growing up was supposed to be like. Not being passed around in a broken system with social workers forgetting about me and misplacing me, but actually feeling cared about. So I finished school, saved for college, and got my degree in elementary education because I wanted to help children."

Evan's eyes are locked on mine. He doesn't look at me with pity, just attentiveness and pure love, making me feel safe to continue.

"That's where I met my husband."

"John," he says, softly.

I nod. "He was also going to school for teaching. He loved football and coaching, and in Texas, high school football is like a religion. He had some great coaches growing up, and it inspired him to become both a coach and teacher."

"It sounds like he was a really good guy."

"He was. The best." The words catch in my throat as a tide of painful memories begin to roll through me. At this point, I don't feel like I can stop until it's all out of me.

I take a deep breath and look at Evan. It's so strange to be talking intimately about John to another man, but I know I love Evan. I love him differently than I loved John, and I think that is what makes me feel guilty. John and I both wanted to create the family that neither of us had growing up. We needed each other.

"We had our ups and downs, but we were happy. Broke newlyweds figuring out new careers and our new marriage. Then I got pregnant."

Evan gently rubs my back. I can see his eyes grow softer with the mention of my pregnancy. His eyes fill with questions and concern.

"I'm sorry I didn't tell you about that," I whisper.

"I think I knew," he said quietly. "I could feel there was more."

"From the moment I discovered I was pregnant, I loved her. Before I even knew her. I was so excited to meet my baby. Emilia Grace."

"That's a beautiful name," he says.

"She was so beautiful," I tell him, my voice cracking. I close my eyes and let myself remember her. As painful as it is, I remember my baby. "I can still smell her newborn smell, feel her warmth in my arms, hear her baby cries..."

When I look up at him, I see he's tearing up, but his eyes never leave mine.

"I loved being Emmie's mom. I loved every minute of it. But I was so tired. Exhausted, I wasn't sleeping, and neither was John..." I hadn't slept more than two hours straight for several weeks. I needed a break so desperately. "Oh, Evan, I'll never forgive myself."

Evan squeezes my hand. Not tightly but firmly. I'm already feeling lighter by finally telling him this.

"I was so overwhelmed and I snapped at John. I just freaked out on him. He needed to run some errands and offered to take her with him. I can still remember the smile on his face as he told me to take a nap. He told me he loved me. Those were his last words to me. I told him I loved him too, that I'd be a new woman when I'd had some sleep, and everything would be fine when they got back."

I shiver and Evan warms me.

"Only… They never came back. I sent them out so that I could take a *nap*. And that's why it's my fault."

"Oh, Beth, no," Evan tries, but I'm not ready to stop.

"I'll never forget a single detail of that day. It's burned into my mind forever. Her '*Congrats! It's a girl!*' balloon hanging limp on the back of my dining room chair. John's contact lens case laying open on the bathroom counter. These simple, day-to-day things that remind us of all we have left."

He holds me closer.

"I fell into bed and thought I had slept for hours, but then I woke with a start. Something was wrong. My heart knew something wasn't right. I looked at my phone and I had only been asleep for twenty-five minutes. I called John right away and he didn't answer. I texted, called more, and nothing."

"How old was Emmie?" Evan asks quietly.

"Three months."

Evan leans into me.

"After, Cara was my rock, answering all of the police's questions, picking me up when I was at my lowest and supporting me however she could. I was inconsolable for a long time, and I felt like the only way to move on was to leave Austin. To leave the place that held all of the memories I shared with my family. The memories we'd never be able to make any more of."

Tears stream down my face. Six years of pent-up sadness, grief, and anger come pouring out of me that I have spent years burying under writing, running, and not getting close to anyone.

It's done. I shared most of it with him. I feel relieved. Spent. Exhausted.

"I'm sorry," Evan says, grazing his lips over the top of my head. "I can't imagine what you've been through."

The warmth of his lips starts to fill the void. The parts of me that died with my family begin to come to life again with his touch. With his love.

"I'm so glad Cara was there with you," he tells me. "That you didn't have to go through that nightmare alone."

My best friend. My sister. She was eight months pregnant, and even after she gave birth to her twins, she still managed to be there for me.

I start shaking, anxious about what he must think about me now. Does he pity me? I don't want anyone's pity. I don't want anyone to feel sorry for me.

I pull away. I don't deserve his love and sympathy. "Do you see now why I can't be with you? Everyone I love dies. My mom, husband, and baby are gone because of me. I can't do that again. I can't bring this kind of pain and messed-up trauma here to you and your family."

Evan shakes his head. "None of that is your fault."

Now I shake mine. "No. I don't deserve anything. I need to

go. I'm sorry. I can't do this. It's just too hard."

I walk back to his cottage and ignore his pleas for me to come back.

I head inside and start packing. I set my bags in the guest room, planning to make a quick exit in the morning with Logan.

I don't belong here. I don't belong anywhere. I need to get back on the move. I will do what Logan wants and take the book deal, but I'll keep moving. I shouldn't have tried to stay here, not when I knew it would never work out.

CHAPTER 24

I won't chase you.

My God, all that pain. That's a lot for someone to carry around. I can understand her hesitation given everything she's been through, but can't she see she's already let me in so much and nothing bad is going to happen? I don't know how to make her see it any more clearly.

All I know is that it can't end like this. I didn't wait twenty-nine years to find my soulmate for her to just leave. She belongs here. I know it and I think she knows it, but she's terrified.

I badly want to go into the guest room, take her in my

arms, and promise to be there for her and try to make her feel better. To let her know that I can't change the past but I can give her a future.

I run into Mellie outside when I take the puppies out to play. She puts down her laundry basket and hugs me.

"What's that for?" I ask when she releases me.

She picks up the basket again and says, "You're a good guy, Evan. Everything you have done for me and Kase? I could never repay you. I am so grateful for you. I don't tell you enough. I wanted you to know it."

While I'm happy to hear this from Mellie, the one I want hugging me and thanking me is Beth. I thought after the transplant I could get the inn all set and life would be just great. Now, I don't even know what I want if I can't have Beth.

"I'm happy you're here. You better not be planning on leaving, too," I say.

Her eyes dart to mine. "She's really leaving?"

"I think so." I glance over at my cottage, feeling frustrated and empty.

I'm a Marine. I save people. I'm a helper. I wanted to help Beth, be her protector, and keep her safe here, but I guess you can't help people who don't want to be helped. She made it clear that she doesn't want to be here.

"I really thought she'd stay," she says.

"I did, too." I fill the puppies' water bowls on the porch.

Just then, Logan comes out. "She texted me that we're leaving. I guess you had the talk?"

"Yeah, that happened."

"Well, what are you going to do about it?" Logan says.

"What *can* I do about it? I can't make her stay. This is her choice."

Logan blinks at me. "I just want her to be happy."

"Oh, yeah, and what will make her happy?" I ask, feeling frustrated. "I can give her this," I say, waving my hand at the inn. "I can love her, give her a family, safety, and security, but apparently that's not enough."

Logan looks away. "You don't get it."

"Then enlighten me so that I can try to fix this!"

"Give her time. What she just told you? I've been waiting six years for that to happen. She has been locked down like Fort Knox. She's never talked about what that grief has done to her and how it has destroyed her. And she let you in, man. She. Let. You. In. Just remember that. She's trying to finally heal. And healing is messy. Stay the course. Don't let her go." He pushes off the porch and strolls over to my cottage.

I'm so tired. I just want her to stay and fight for me the way I'm fighting for her.

Beth soon joins me on the back porch. Her eyes are puffy, her face red. "I have to go," she says, not looking at me.

"Why?" I ask.

"I need to go home to grieve. I never let myself properly

grieve and heal."

I nodded. "And why can't you do that here?"

"I need to go home," she says quietly, unable to look at me.

"This *is* home, Beth. Don't you feel that here? We feel it with you. I feel it with you. You belong here."

The look on her face guts me. It's pure anguish. She just stares at the ground, not saying anything.

I repeat the question. "Why can't you heal here?"

"I need to go home and face everything. I can't keep running anymore."

"Looks to me like you're still running."

"I'm sorry; I don't know how not to."

"Why won't you let me help you?"

"You've helped me more than you'll ever know."

"Then why are you leaving? Am I not enough?"

"That's not it at all. It's truly not you, it's me."

"That sounds like an excuse, Beth. You want to go back to Austin? I'll take you."

She shakes her head, tears streaming down her cheeks. "I can't take you up on that."

"Why the hell not?" My voice cracks. I'm upset, but I'm trying really hard not to lose it right now.

"You don't understand."

"Then make me understand! You're just going to throw us away like this?"

Her eyes finally look over and meet mine. They're full of tears, matching my own. "I'm not sure I even understand it," she says.

I can no longer contain my anger. "I guess I can't lose someone I never really had. You've told me from the beginning you wouldn't stay; I guess I shouldn't have thought I could change your mind. All along, this was just bullshit, wasn't it?" I know I'm probably pushing it, but I can't stop myself.

Logan carries her bags out to his SUV. His head is down, trying not to acknowledge me.

Even feeling the way I do now, I still have no regrets that we were together. I would rather have loved her for a little than never have loved her at all, but I can't tell her that in my current state. Instead, I snap.

"Fine. Just go. I don't deserve this. And neither do you. We could have been forever, Beth," I say quietly.

Beth looks like she's in so much pain and I can't stand it. I want to hold her, tell her everything is going to be okay, and be there for her. I want to tell her that I hated running this inn every single day until she showed up. That I can't imagine not having her here by my side.

But I'm upset and I'm angry, so I can't tell her that. All I can tell her is, "I don't want this."

She doesn't respond, just silently cries.

I take a deep breath. "If you leave, I won't chase you. I love you. Do you hear me? I said it, I'll say it again, and I mean it. I know what I want," I say, pointing at my chest. "I want you. All of you. The good, the bad, and anything else you've got."

She's shaking now. I want to console her, but I can't. I can't make her want me back.

I fight back my own tears. "But I won't chase you," I say quietly.

The look Beth gives me tears me to shreds. "I want to love you like you love me, but I don't know if I can. You deserve better than I can give you."

"Just go," I say quietly, feeling defeated.

CHAPTER 25

Beth

What happened in Freedom Valley?

"Are you sure you want to do this?"

I nod, unable to form words right now. I lean my face against the cold car window and cry as Logan pulls away. I cry until I don't think I have anything left in me.

"I think you're making a mistake," he says as he turns off onto the highway. "I think he really loves you, Beth. All these people seem to love you."

"I don't deserve them."

"I think you can't let yourself be fully loved by anyone

else until you first love yourself."

He's probably right, but right now, I'm so tired. I just need to get away. It's what I do; I run. It probably doesn't make sense to anyone—even I don't understand it—but it's how I have coped.

Logan's house in Boston is a construction zone and now I remember why he was staying at The Golden Gable. I ruined that for him, too. Great.

"I'm sorry. I forgot about your floors. I can find a hotel."

"The floors are done upstairs. Come on."

I set my stuff up in his guest room and call Cara. "Where are you?" she asks.

"At Logan's. I think I destroyed everything, Cara. I told Evan everything."

"Wait... Everything?"

"Yeah," I said quietly. "Everything."

"That's huge, Beth. That's progress. But, what happened? Why are you in Boston and not with Evan?"

"I can't do it, Cara. I can't be with him."

"Oh, Beth. Come home to Austin. Let me book you a flight."

I put my face in my hands as panic fills my chest.

"It'll be fine. Come here and let us take care of you."

"Okay."
"I'll be there for you."'
"You always are, thank you."

My plane touches down in Austin a day later. I feel like I'm torn between two worlds, like my family is here in Austin with John and Emmie, but my heart is in Freedom Valley with people are alive and breathing and still able to love me back. I don't know how to stop feeling like I'm betraying my family if I move on.

I sling my backpack over my shoulder. I didn't pack much because I didn't have the time or energy to deal with packing before my flight. I head outside to wait for Cara, who pulls up in her white SUV within minutes. I jump in and lean over to hug her tight.

"I've missed you," I tell her.

"We've missed you. The twins are excited you're coming." She sizes me up. "You look sad but good."

It's been over a year since Cara, Steve, and their twin girls visited Logan in Boston and I joined everyone for the weekend. This is the first time I've been back to Austin in a very long time.

I slide my glasses back up my nose and we drive for a while. The closer we get to our small town, the stronger the magnetic pull I feel toward them. I need her to stop.

"Can we make a stop?" I ask.

She looks over at me and quietly nods. "Of course."

I don't even have to tell her where she needs to stop, because sometimes you have friends that just know. And Cara knows; she always has. She pulls into the cemetery and drives until she gets to where they are.

She unbuckles her seatbelt, but I put my hand on hers. "Can I do this alone for a minute?"

"I'll be here."

I find the Covey headstone with John Michael on one side and Emilia Grace on the other. I run my fingers over the letters and tears slide down my cheeks. I kneel in front and smooth the flowers. Cara has told me that many of John's former players, students, and parents have visited. This makes me feel worse that I haven't been here.

"I'm so sorry. I love you both so much." My voice trembles. "I'm so sorry I haven't been back. I'm just so sorry. I'm sorry this happened. I wish you were both here.

"I miss you so much," I whisper. I sit and pull my legs to my chest, wrapping my arms around them, pulling them closer.

My mind goes back to that day again. My heart in my chest feels like it's going to explode as I allow the memories to flow in instead of avoiding them like I've done a good job of doing for the past six years.

My mind goes back to the highway that day when we came upon the wreck. I remember getting out and running up to the EMT who was blocking traffic with his ambulance. I looked inside the ambulance, expecting to see my family, but it was empty. I asked him who had been involved in the wreck. I explained frantically that I couldn't get ahold of my husband because he wasn't answering his phone but his last location was here on this highway.

I'll never forget the EMT's face as he looked over to the county deputy standing nearby. He was young and scared. He wouldn't look directly at me. I stared hard, searching his face, hoping he'd finally acknowledge me and tell me that it was someone else, but he couldn't meet my eyes.

Finally, the deputy approached, a grave expression on his face. That was the moment that changed my life. I knew.

I can still remember the sharp pain in my chest. The way he looked at me, I'll never forget. He knew there were no words he could say to make this any easier. There was no easy way for him to tell me what I needed to be told. My heart still breaks for that deputy.

I remember the air leaving my body as I tried to keep from falling apart. I tried to look around him, but he moved to block my view so I couldn't see. I remember asking him, "Is it bad? What happened?" I pleaded with him for any information.

I mentally prepared myself for whatever we needed to

do—rehab, a long hospital stay, we'd do whatever it took—but nothing could prepare me for what he was about to say.

"We found no survivors, ma'am," he answered solemnly.

"Can you keep looking? I can help you," I had answered, not understanding.

"I'm sorry, they're gone. Is there anyone we can call for you?" he asks, his face trying to be strong, but I could tell this was very hard for him.

Cara ran up at that moment and I collapsed to the pavement next to her. That moment rocked me to my core. It broke something in me that I don't think I can ever get back. My family was gone. My entire world. My reason for living... Gone. That day, that moment, everything changed for me. Some things you just never get over.

I sit and pull my knees to my chest. I remember walking into our home after that and it suddenly felt like someone else's, like right out of a nightmare. Like seeing our home from a different person. Which makes sense now, because I was a different person after that. Emmie's stroller was still in the front hallway, parked and ready for her next evening walk that John and I took every night with her. There were reminders everywhere I looked. I just wanted the pain to go away.

I packed the pain away and ran for six years.

And now, I'm home again. And I think it's finally time to heal.

I cry until I feel exhausted. I needed this. I feel them with me wherever I go, but I don't feel them here at the grave as I thought I would. It makes me feel better to know that they have been with me the past six years no matter where I've been.

"John, I hope you're taking care of our baby girl. Give her a big hug and kiss for me. I miss you. Coming back here is hard. I see all the memories we made together, and I would give anything to have you here."

After a while, I head back to the car, knowing I'll be back often while I'm here in Austin. "Thanks," I say as I slide in and shut my door.

"Are you good?" Cara asks.

"I think I will be. It's time. It's been a long time. I thought time would make it better. But honestly? I don't think it will truly ever get better unless I face it and work to process it. I can't keep running and burying it under work."

"I'm proud of you, and I love you. You know you're always welcome here, anytime, for however long."

"Thanks," I tell her. "I'm ready."

We drive in silence back to her house. When we pull into the driveway and I see her white house with black shutters, I immediately feel a pang in my chest. I remember coming here with John all the time.

Everly and Grace come running out and give me a hug. Cara was pregnant with her girls when Emmie and John died. My eyes sting because Emmie wouldn't be that much older than them if she had lived. I think about that all the time when Cara sends pictures. How would she have liked kindergarten? What would her favorite foods be? What toys would she be playing with? I miss her. I've missed everything.

"Hey, girls." I hug them back then grab my backpack.

"Come on, love. Steve has the grill going. We're going to get relaxed, get some wine, and it's going to be okay."

Later, we sit outside in the warm Texas fall and talk.

Cara sips her wine. "What happened in Freedom Valley?" she asks.

"Did you talk to Logan?"

"Yeah, I did. He likes Evan. He says he seems like a great guy, and he's confused what happened. I'm confused, too. Why did you leave?"

Why did I leave? Because it hurts. I could lose him, too, and I'm scared to hurt again. I know I sound crazy when I actually say it out loud.

I take a deep breath. "He told me he loves me. I couldn't say it back. I just feel like I have so much to work through before I can go there... I don't know if I can ever go there again with someone else. I just got scared."

"So you think it's easier *not* to love again?"

"Maybe," I say as I look out over the yard. Seeing the twins' toys scattered everywhere makes me miss Kase.

"That doesn't make sense."

"I know, but I still feel it."

"What's holding you back?"

I explain to her how I felt about my heart still feeling there but guilty about my family here.

"They're not here. They're still with you wherever you go. They're a part of you. I think when you are able to understand that they're not here, to let go of the idea of them being here somehow because you lost them here, you'll be able to move on."

I know she's right about that, but what she doesn't get just yet is that Evan is also gone. "It's done with Evan," I tell her. "He said he won't chase me. He was really mad when I left. Really mad."

"Well, guess what? People get mad. That doesn't mean they're completely done with someone. Especially not when he told you he loves you. He has to see that you have a lot you're working through right now."

"He has his own things to worry about." I think about the fall festival happening soon and my heart sinks. I'm going to miss it. I miss them. I miss him.

"One day at a time. One hour, one minute at a time, if you need it. Don't give up on him. I don't think he's giving up on you."

Evan's words echo in my head. He won't come for me. He's done.

I shake my head. "You didn't hear the things he said when I left."

"Just take it one day at a time…"

The next day goes by in a blur. I walk through our old home. The property management company had it painted and changed the floors, but the place still holds so many memories. Good and then bad. I've decided to list it for sale and move forward. It's funny to think I've owned a house all these years and rented it out when most of that time I was homeless. The irony is not lost on me. Sometimes living when the ones you love have died is harder than dying. Navigating life alone has been the hardest thing I've ever done.

I drive by the old school where I taught and think of my students, how they'd be in fifth grade now. I think of my own little girl and what class she'd be in. We could have gone to school together and I would have been home with her on all our school breaks.

I remember John and I dreaming about taking an old school bus and turning it into a travel bus, spending our summer breaks traveling all over the U.S. exploring. I dreamed of a sticker map that we'd fill it with all of the states we'd visit and the memories we'd make with our kids. All memories that would never be.

I drive by the high school football field where I watched John coach countless games. He loved those kids so much, and they loved him. So many people lost out the day that drunk driver killed my family and herself. We'll never know how many lives he would have impacted as a coach, teacher, father, husband, and friend.

Finally, I head to the storage unit where everything's packed away. I take a deep breath before lifting the door. I stand back and take it all in, the unit full of furniture and boxes of memories that I have to sift through and take care of.

Bags and bags and bags of clothes. Bins full of holiday decor I lovingly decorated our home with.

Many people mistakenly thought I won a big settlement from the driver. But she was a repeat offender and she only had crappy, bare bones coverage because of her previous violations. She had no assets, no home, nothing. I got a $50,000 payout, of which the lawyer took 33.3 percent. What was left didn't even cover the funerals. I wiped out our savings to give them both proper burials and managed to walk away with $9,000 worth of debt that took me years to pay off.

I realize I don't want anything in the storage unit. Not now. I know that coming to acknowledge the stuff here was a step in the right direction, but I can't do this today.

I grab a coffee and head back to the cemetery. I need to talk to my husband. I need to tell him about the man I love, even if he probably doesn't love me back anymore.

CHAPTER 26

Evan

She's lost.
And you need to go find her.

I bang the drawer of the cash register shut. I'm still angry—I've been angry since she left—and it's showing. I'm short with guests, I sleep every chance I get, and I don't feel like doing anything but brooding and getting pissed at everyone.

Really, I'm pissed at myself, but no one needs to know that. My mom is flying back from San Diego tonight, so she'll probably know it, but she's also probably going to be pissed herself that Beth isn't here and she didn't have a chance to say goodbye.

Pete enters the front room then looks around for guests before hissing at me. "Enough. You're acting like a little asshole and we're all sick of it." He gives me a look that your CO gives you when he's about to light you up. Pete never talks to me like this, nor has he ever looked at me like this, so I know what he is telling me must definitely be true.

"Come on, let's go," he says as he yanks open the front door and yells out, "Sash, I've got Evan for a while."

She comes down the hall, drying her hands on a towel. "Thank God," she states and glares at me, then heads back to the kitchen.

"Great," I mumble as I grab my coat and follow Pete outside to his truck.

"Get in."

I feel like I'm getting scolded by my dad. God, I miss him. I'd give anything for him to yell at me right now.

Pete grumbles something incoherent as he starts driving.

"Where are we going?" I ask him.

"We're driving. I've been told not to bring you back until I talk some sense into you."

I hang my head. "I'm sorry. I know I've been angry."

I can't help it. I feel so much despair. I miss her so much. I turn in the night to hold her and she's not there. Even the puppies remind me of her. Everywhere I turn now, there are reminders of her. Nothing is the same without her.

"You've been downright awful," Pete tells me. "And you want to know the worst part?"

I just look at him because I know what's coming.

"You did this," he says simply. "You."

Okay, that wasn't what I expected. "Me? I didn't freaking leave, Pete. She left! She doesn't want me. She made her choice."

"Do you really think that woman is capable of making a rational choice right now, with everything she's been through? She's lost, and you need to go find her."

"I can't. I don't even know where she is."

"You know where she is. Your heart knows. Me and Sasha booked you a ticket. Monday, after the festival. You're going to Austin. Figure it out."

"I don't know…" I hedge.

"And you're not freaking coming back without her. You know she belongs here. I'd go to the moon to get Sasha back if she left. Don't be a dumbass."

I pull my head up and look at him. "But what if I can't get her to come back?"

"Well, asshole, you hid her car in your barn and it's still there."

I smile and shake my head, realizing she has to come back for her car eventually.

"Jesus, thank the lord," he says, rolling his eyes.

"What?"

"That's the first time anyone has ever seen you smile in days."

He does a U-turn then drives us back to the inn. When he pulls up to the front, he asks, "Is your head out of your ass?"

"Yeah."

"Good. Get out of my truck."

I walk up to the inn with a little more resolve. I know what I need to do now.

Everything is ready for the fall festival tomorrow, and I'm excited to see how it all turns out.

I head to the garden shed where we do laundry with a pile of my clothes and start a load. I turn to find Mellie standing there, her eyes narrowed at me.

I know I'm about to have my ass handed to me again, and I welcome it. "Come on," I say. "Let's have it." I lean back against the washer and look up at the ceiling, waiting.

She doesn't hold back. "I know you're my boss and I shouldn't be so forward, but I'm going to just tell you like it is. I think it's dumb and prideful that you said you wouldn't chase her. We're not in elementary school, Evan. You need to go get her."

"You done?" I ask. I cross my arms and lean toward her, smiling.

I love that Beth left an impression on this inn. Everyone misses her and loves her. This isn't lost on me; I need to make this right.

"Yeah. I miss her." Her face relaxes and she drops her shoulders. "She was so kind to Kase and me, and I feel like I finally made a friend."

My heart clenches. Mellie did need a friend. She has been more open and relaxed since Beth came. It took a long time to get Mellie to trust my mom and me, and for her to trust and miss Beth is a big deal.

"I miss her, too. I'm going to get her."

She huffs. "Way to bury the lede."

"And miss out on that performance? Not on your life."

Mellie throws a towel at me and heads out, but I don't miss the smile that reaches her eyes before she goes.

I head out to do my nightly rounds. Tomorrow is going to be so busy and I want to make sure everything is all set.

Before I check the grounds, I head to my mom's cottage to open it up and make sure it's ready for her since she's been gone a while. I know she's loved being with Allie and Caleb, but she misses being home, too. Caleb is finally out of the hospital and he's doing amazing. I'm so damn proud of that kid. He's a fighter.

Pete drops my mom off just as I'm walking back outside.

"Mom," I say, giving her a hug.

"It's so good to be home, honey. I'm so tired of

traveling."

"Thanks, Pete," I say with a wave as he pulls out and heads home to his own cottage.

"Come in for a while, honey," she tells me. "I need a cup of tea and I want to hear what's been going on."

"I'm going to turn in for an early day tomorrow, Mom. Did Pete fill you in?"

"He did. I'm glad you're going to her."

"I'm not sure she's going to come back."

"You have to try. None of that 'I'm not chasing you' nonsense."

"I know. I messed up."

"You'll make it better. It'll be okay." She pats my cheek. "Trim this beard first, though. You're getting kind of scruffy."

"Thanks, Mom." I rub my hand over my beard then head out to finish my tasks for tomorrow. It's going to be a long day with the festival and my body still isn't quite healed.

CHAPTER 27

Evan

Where's Beth?

It's over an hour before my alarm is set to go off, but I finally give up on sleep and just get up. I shower quickly, throwing on jeans and a flannel. I head over to the main inn and start coffee.

It's my favorite time when the inn is quiet and I have the place to myself. I take my steaming mug back to my office and turn on my computer. I stare at the screen for a long time before I realize I'm staring at nothing and can't concentrate.

None of this is the same without her. I'm excited for the

fall festival today, but she should be here. She did most of the work for this and she can't even be around to enjoy it. It feels wrong.

I hear Sasha moving around the kitchen so I head back and check in with her.

"Ready for today?" I ask as I slide into one of the bar stools.

"You're up early," she says, her tone terse. "I see you got the coffee on."

"I couldn't sleep."

She finally looks at me and softens. "What time did the vendors finish setting up last night?"

"Around nine," I tell her. "But it's all ready for them under the tent now. They can just show up and open up."

She leans her elbows on the counter and narrows her eyes at me. "Pete says he has a surprise for me. He better not have anything that shoots or blows anything up."

I shrug my shoulders and look away. Oh, it's going to be great to see what happens when Pete brings out the pumpkin cannon.

"I'm making biscuits and gravy for the guests and staff," Sasha says.

"Sounds good. I'm going to let the dogs out for a walk and feed them. I'll be back in a bit."

The puppies whimper as I head to their kennel and let them out. They sniff me and Chip looks at me with disdain.

"I know, I know, buddy. I miss her, too. I'm going to get her back for you." Damn it. Even the dogs are protesting.

The festival finally gets started, and I dodge no less than a dozen questions just in the first hour about where Beth is and when she'll be back. I can tell she poured her heart into this festival and it's not just me who has fallen in love with Beth. The whole town of Freedom Valley has. I realize she had pretty much made friends and connected with every single vendor, and the disappointment was strong when everyone learned she wasn't here. I didn't miss the looks I got.

I walk by the food vendors and grab a caramel apple from Kameron, one of the baristas from The Freedom Bean. "Hey, man, how are you?" I ask.

"Hey, Evan, did I tell you I enlisted?" he asks.

"What? No, you didn't. What branch?"

"Army, like my grandpa. But you inspired me with your time in the Marines."

"Congratulations, buddy," I say as I clap him on his back. "I'm so proud of you. When do you head out?"

"After the first of the year."

"You'll do great. Let me know if you want to get a few workouts in with me before you go."

"That would be awesome, man."

"Proud of you." I head over to the caramel popcorn and buy a bag. I scoop a handful in my mouth and savor the flavors—salty and sweet—and the fresh kernels just melt in my mouth. It's so good. In fact, aside from the thousand questions about Beth, everything is good today. Music is playing and people are milling around, shopping and having a great time. If my dad was here, he'd be visiting and laughing right along with them. The success of the festival makes me happy.

I head through the festival which has been planned down to the tiniest details and staffed with volunteers. It runs so smoothly that even my dad would be impressed, and he ran the annual fall festival here at the inn for decades. People joked he was like Taylor Doose from *Gilmore Girls*, only a friendlier version. I never watched the show, but I've heard it from several people, even down to the goofy hat and bow tie he wore.

The aroma of kettle corn, funnel cakes, and coffee fills the air. Laughter, chatter, and kids having fun in the corn maze are like music to my ears.

I hear a loud bang and follow it to the back field where I spot Sasha scolding Pete, who's standing with half a dozen other guys as they launch pumpkins across the field with the pumpkin cannon he created. They roar and high five each time a pumpkin launches and crashes to the ground in pieces. "This is not funny!" Sasha shrieks.

Pete seems to disagree; he roars with laughter.

He then hugs Sasha and kisses her on the cheek. She looks

like she's impressed but trying to hide it.

My mom joins me. She's holding a mug of coffee with our Golden Gable Inn logo on it, wearing an orange shirt that reads, "Freedom Valley Fall Fest."

"Nice shirt. Where did you get it?" I ask.

"Beth had them made. They're over there." She points to a booth in the corner. "I saw one with your name on it."

My heart races as I head over and find a box in the back with, sure enough, a shirt in my size with my name pinned to it. There's a heart drawn under my name. She must have done this before she got upset and left. I switch out my shirts and put this one on under my open flannel.

When I come back to where I left my mom, she smiles at me and says, "Hey, honey, the airplane candy drop is scheduled for three. The kids are so excited." She explains that a neighbor's taking his crop duster plane over the clearing for the candy drop.

"How did they come up with that? It's genius."

Kase runs by with Ninja Turtle face paint on and shrieks, "Hi, Evan! Cowabunga, dude!"

"Beth did all of this," my mom responds. "We've had over five hundred people come through here so far today, and we still have tomorrow, too."

"This is incredible."

As I scan the festival, so many memories of my dad come back to me. Some I may have tucked down deep inside because it hurt to remember. Grief is never easy. I think of Beth and her enormous loss and the grief I know she has felt for the past six years. How did she function enough to create all this? It's like, without even realizing it, she brought a piece of my dad back here that we were missing. My dad would have loved seeing all of this. And he would have loved Beth.

I head over to where Sam and his band are playing and he motions to me to grab a guitar and join them for a while. I do, and it feels good. It puts a smile on my face, and for a brief moment, I almost forget her. Almost. But it's impossible when every love song makes me miss her. Then, Sam suggests we play "You Are The Reason" by Calum Scott, and the lyrics hit me in the gut.

CHAPTER 28

I won't forget this.

The festival was a huge hit. Not only did we make a ton of money, we also had so many new bookings. So much of the community came out and showed their support. It was something my dad would have been so proud of.

We're still short on cash for Hamilton, but we're getting closer. We're definitely in a completely different place than where we were.

Before Beth came into our lives.

The thought of Beth missing the festival squeezes my heart. I'm going to do my best to make sure she never misses another one.

When my phone goes off, I'm surprised to see it's Preston calling.

"I'm sorry to call you so late, but I wanted to update you on a few things," he tells me.

"Sure, no problem."

"First, we were planning to have your loan transferred to another bank. But before I could present that option to you, an anonymous donor actually paid off the loan in full."

The loan was paid off? By who?

"This means you no longer have any business ties with Hamilton McGraw. My sources also tell me that the bank board isn't happy with the way he's handled this situation, and that he's likely going to be fired."

I can't believe what I'm hearing, but I need to know. I press for more details, but all he says is, "I can't tell you who. It's strictly confidential."

I take a deep breath and exhale a sigh of relief. But in that relief that our problems are finally over, I also know we can't take this money. It doesn't seem right. "We can't accept this Preston, that's too much."

"It's a done deal, Evan."

"So the bank can't take the inn."

"Nope. You're all safe. The inn is paid in full and you're debt free."

"Thank you." I'm in shock. I sit, running my hand

nervously through my beard. Am I dreaming?

"I'm happy it all worked out. Also, I wanted to let you know that I'm opening up a small practice in Freedom Valley. So if you need anything, just let me know." I like Preston. I'm glad he'll be sticking around. I wonder if Mellie would like him…

"I will. I won't forget this. Thank you."

It's over. It's finally over. Our inn is safe. Caleb is going to be okay. Everything is okay. Now, there's just one thing left to save.

I find Sasha and my mom at the kitchen table, drinking tea in their robes. My mom smiles at me warmly and Sasha gives me a side eye.

"You do know I can see you when you look at me like that?"

"You know what you need to do."

"Stop it, you two," my mom shoots back. "He's going to get her tomorrow. And he's not coming back without her, right?" She stares at me.

"That's the plan," I say. "I can't kidnap her."

"She belongs here with us, and you know it," Sasha says. "You shouldn't have let her leave in the first place."

I explain to Sasha and my mom about Beth and what happened with John and Emmie. After I finish, both are crying.

My mom can hardly speak. "I knew she was a widow,

but I didn't know she was a mother," she manages. "I can't imagine. I just want to hug her. I miss her so much." She shuffles toward me and gives me a hug before saying goodnight and heading home.

Sasha's tone softens and she says, "You and her are it. Don't mess this up, Evan."

"Thanks, Sash. I'm going to bring her home."

CHAPTER 29

I know she can feel me.
I can feel it.

My plane touches down in Austin. I'm nervous but I text Cara, glad I thought to get her contact info from Logan.

> **Evan**: Cara, this is Evan. I'm in Austin. Can you help me find Beth?

I hope she'll help me, given that she doesn't even know me. I'm hoping maybe Beth told her some good things about me.

I look down at my phone and keep checking for a response and finally there it is.

Cara: Where are you?

Evan: The airport.

Cara: Do you have a ride?

Evan: No, I wasn't sure where she was staying.

Cara: She's staying with us. You can stay with us, too. Wait there, I'm going to have Steve come get you.

Evan: Thank you.

Cara: Steve is on his way. Silver car. It will take about thirty minutes for him to get there. I'll text you his contact info.

Evan: Do you think she'll take me back? She left so angry.

Cara: I honestly don't know. But what I can tell you is that she's in a better place now than when she got here.

I go find a place to plug in my phone and I wait for what seems like forever. I'm really second guessing all of this. I show up in a city, not sure where she is, hoping her friend will help me. This could go a completely different way than I want it to and Beth might reject me.

My phone rings. After Cara and I say our hellos, I ask flatly, "Does she know I'm here in Austin or that you're talking to me?"

"No. But I have questions before you get here," she says, her voice soft. I can tell she's hesitant. I would be, too.

"Do you think she even wants to see me?" I ask.

"Beth never grieved like she probably should have after her family was killed. This is a long time coming. Don't give up on her. She just needs time."

That's just what Logan said. Now I really understand, they're right. "I miss her," I tell Cara. "So much. Everyone back home does."

"She misses you. I can tell she's trying not to because she has so much to process. The pain from the past, the future you could be for her."

"I want to be there for her and help her in any way that I can."

"I think it's going to be okay. I'm glad we're finally getting to meet you."

"Thanks for all of your help, Cara."

I hang up, noticing the time, and I head outside to meet Steve.

Within minutes, he pulls up and I wave him down. I climb into the passenger

seat. "Good to meet you. We don't get a lot of lumberjack-looking guys like you around here."

"Lumberjack?" I look down at my flannel and scratch my beard. Right.

"Cara tells me you're here to get your girl back."

Steve's a big guy with a beard and a teddy bear vibe. I can see why Beth loves these people. They seem really great.

He pulls away from the curb and asks me if I want a drink or to stop for anything.

"I just need to see her."

"Understandable. I'll take you to her."

"Where is she?"

"Cara tracked her location on her Find My Friends app, and it looks like she's at the cemetery. I'm going to drop you off there, if that's okay?"

I nod and take a deep breath. "Yeah. Definitely." I'm nervous to see her, but I miss her so much.

"So you knew John?" I ask.

He was quiet for a bit then finally lets out a soft, "Yeah. He was a great guy."

"Any words of advice?"

"Just love her, man. Don't complicate things. Just love her through this. It'll work out."

He turns into the cemetery and drives up a hill before parking behind a white SUV.

My heart cracks when I look up and see Beth up on the hill, sitting on the ground, her long blonde hair falling in waves down her back.

I nod. "I'll be okay. You don't have to wait. Thank you."

"Totally fine. Give me a wave when you're ready," he says.

I get out of the car and head up the hill. My heart is beating so fast. It feels like it's in my throat and I can't breathe. As I get closer, I can feel her pain radiating from her. I can feel her sadness with every step. All I want is to wrap her in a big hug and never let her go.

I know she can feel me, but she doesn't move. Her shoulders shake slightly and I can tell she's crying. She's talking to them.

I look back and wave at Steve; he waves then drives off.

I carefully sit down behind her and scoot up around her. I pull her close to me and tuck her under my chin, just holding her. She never turns back to look at me, but her body relaxes and she sinks into mine, making relief flood through me. She wants me here and that's all I need to know; I hold her tight and kiss her cheek.

CHAPTER 30

Beth

No more maybes for us.

I can feel him approach; I know it's him. The air around me changes as it always does when he's near. It feels calmer, safer, and electric. In a good way.

I take a deep breath when I feel him slide in behind me and pull me close, wrapping his arms around me.

I was telling my family about him and thinking about some funny memories that we had together before they died. And then he came. He said he wouldn't come, but here he is.

I lean back into him and take a deep breath. We sit like this for probably a half an hour. Just calm. Still.

Finally, he wipes my tears with the sleeve of his soft flannel and kisses my cheek. He has his cap on backwards and he leans in and pulls me tight, not saying anything. Just being here with me in this moment, the hot Texas wind blowing gently around us.

I lean in and finally murmur, "You came."

He nods but doesn't say anything.

"You said you wouldn't chase me."

"Some things are worth chasing, Beth. You're worth it. We're worth it. We both deserve this." He nods to their headstone. "They would want you to be happy."

"I had to tell them about you."

He doesn't say anything but his arms flex around me. "Tell me about them. Introduce me."

"I can't forget them."

He hugs me tighter. "Emmie and John will never be forgotten. Our children will know them, our family will know them, we will all celebrate and love them."

Tears flow again but these are tears of relief and happiness. I wasn't sure how I could merge my two worlds, but somehow, I just know it will work out. It might be messy and painful at times, but it's going to be okay.

I lean back into him. "John, meet Evan. Evan, meet John."

"I'll take care of her, I promise," he says quietly.

"Thank you for coming for me," I say, turning around and getting lost in his green eyes.

"I will always come for you, Beth. Always." He leans in and kisses my neck.

A little bit later, we walk down the hill and I stop and look back.

"What's wrong?" he asks.

"I don't want to leave them."

"We'll never leave them. We'll come back as often as you want."

"Okay."

We get into Cara's borrowed SUV. I look at him and just smile. "I'm so glad you're here."

"Me too." He leans in and kisses me.

"Are you hungry?" I ask.

"I'm starving."

"I know a place."

We end up at a diner called Tillie's and slide into a booth across from each other. A server comes over and hands us our menus.

I reach over and squeeze his arm. He stands up then scoots in beside me, putting his arm around me so we can look at the menu together. I love that he wants to be near me. I never want to leave him again.

"I have to ask you something," he says.

"What?" I say as I scan the menu.

"Did you pay off the loan for the inn?" he asks, his eyes softly searching mine.

I don't look at him but my eyes widen slightly. "Why would you ask that?"

"Did you?" he asks again, gently.

Finally, I say, "I'd do anything for you and the inn. I love you. I love all of you."

His eyes soften. "I love you, too."

"I know you don't want to accept it, but it's a done deal. You did so much for me, Evan. The inn, your family. I can never fully explain it, but you all... You saved me. You reminded me that I wasn't fully living and that I could be... I could be loved again. And for that, I can never repay all of you."

"There's no payment needed when it's family. It's just what we do for each other, Beth. You didn't have to do that."

I lean my head on his shoulder. *Damn, I love this man.* "I know. But it's done. It's safe."

"How did you do it? That's so much money," he asks.

"I got a book deal with Logan. It's okay, I promise."

He shakes his head gently but pulls me tighter.

"How're Allie and Caleb?" I ask, intentionally trying to change the subject.

"Doing well. Caleb's recovering and Allie is back to working from home. My mom's back in town, too."

"Ah, good. I wondered who was running things while you're here."

Our server returns then and we order a local special called the slopper, fries, and milkshakes. Chocolate, of course. The slopper is a burger topped in a green chili sauce and eaten with a fork. Evan looks skeptical, but I assure him it's good.

"Is this a special place for you?" he asks.

I pause and allow the memories to flood through me.

"John and I came here after games to celebrate with his team and their families, win or lose. This is a pretty special small town. It has a lot of memories."

A family sitting across from us keeps staring and I finally recognize the little boy as one I had in class. I remember after John and Emmie died, the family had sent flowers and a card. This town had so much love for our family. Now I feel bad that I stayed away all those years.

The mom stands and she and the boy come over to us. "Mrs. Covey, I thought that was you," the boy tells me.

"Hi, Matthew, it's good to see you. What grade are you in now?"

"Fifth."

"You have grown up!" I turn to his mom. "How are you doing?"

"We're great. It's so good to see you. We knew you left town but didn't know where you had moved to."

"I've traveled for a while, but Freedom Valley, New

Hampshire is home now," I say as I squeeze Evan's hand under the table. His gorgeous green eyes shine.

She smiles. "Well, don't be a stranger. We sure do miss you around here. Good seeing you!"

"Good seeing you, Mrs. Covey," Matthew says with a smile as they head back to their table.

Seeing a past student makes me miss teaching. I wonder if I should go back to it. I can write, too. But, I do miss my students. Coming here and working on my healing has definitely reminded me of a lot of the things I used to love and let go of due to painful memories.

One of the things I've realized in the past few days is that I can stop focusing on the pain and instead choose to focus on the positive memories we had. John wouldn't want me to be sad. He would want me to be happy.

I look up at Evan. "I love you."

He looks intently at me now and says, "I knew from day one I was going to love you."

"I think I knew it, too. It just took me longer to believe it, to believe it could work with the mess of my life."

"Life is messy, Beth. Embrace it." The food arrives then, and he immediately takes a big bite of his food.

"What's the plan after this?"

"You tell me. I'm here. The inn is safe. Caleb is healthy. I have you back… almost. What's next?"

I look at him and think for a minute. "I want you to meet

Cara and her family. They're so important to me. Aside from Logan, they're the only family I have..."

"Besides us at home..." He smiles.

Home. I like that I have a home now. "Wait a minute, how did you find me and figure out where I was?"

He grinned. "Steve and Cara. I texted Cara from the airport and Steve came to get me."

"Oh good. I'm glad I get to finally share you with them."

"Glad to meet them."

Just then, I realize something huge I missed back home at the inn. "Oh my gosh! How was the festival? Tell me everything."

"A huge success, thanks to you and your hard work. Everyone misses you. Apparently the town has voted you the unofficial mayor."

"I miss them all, too. Do you think they'll be surprised when I come back?"

"Well, I'll put it this way. If I don't bring you home with me, I probably just shouldn't ever go home again. They're pretty mad at me."

I frown at the thought of his family being mad at him. "I'm sorry I missed the festival."

"You can be at every other one from here on out."

"Deal."

"And the puppies miss you," he says, dragging a fry through ketchup.

My chest swells. "I have to take care of some things here first, but I'll come back with you."

"I'll help you," he says as he looks at me, his sea green eyes reaching mine.

"I love you."

"I love you, maybe more."

"No more maybes for us," he says, pulling me closer.

CHAPTER 31

Evan

Do you think there's room for me?

I hold Beth's hand as we enter Cara and Steve's home. They're in the kitchen and their girls are at the counter coloring.

Cara hugs me immediately. "It's so great to finally meet you." Then she turns to Beth and mouths, "He's so hot."

Beth grins as she shrugs her shoulders and says, "I know."

Steve rolls his eyes and nudges me. "So, it looks like things went well?"

"They did. Thanks again for coming to get me," I tell him.

"No problem. Want a beer? I'm going to fire up the grill in a little bit."

"Actually, I'll take a water if I can? Supposed to lay off alcohol now that I'm down to one kidney." I smile as I motion to my abdomen.

"Oh, yeah! I forgot you had just had a kidney out. You look pretty good for someone who just had surgery," Cara says.

"Thanks, I'm still getting around a little slower than usual but it's going well. I'm just glad my nephew's doing so much better now."

We head out to the patio and watch the twins play on their swing set. Cara and Beth settle in together while Steve and I check out the barbeque.

"You think there's room for me?" I ask. I watch Beth show Cara something on her phone and they laugh.

"Definitely, brother. Definitely." He clanks his beer against my water glass.

This is Beth's world. She's seen mine, and now I get to see hers. I'm so relieved that she's finally fully letting me in.

CHAPTER 32

Beth

So what's the plan?

I watch as Evan sits out on the patio with Steve. I glance over at Cara and she smiles. "You needed this," she tells me. "You needed him."

"I can't believe he came all the way to Austin for me."

"Well, I think it's safe to say he'd probably go to the ends of the earth for you."

"It feels good to have someone to love again; someone who loves me back."

"Well, you better get used to it. He looks pretty comfortable around you."

"Is it weird seeing him here when it used to be John and the baby here with me?"

She looks thoughtful for a second before she responds, "No. We miss John and Emmie, and that'll never change. But things happen and we can't help that; we just have to take the good and celebrate that. Evan's the new good, but that won't take away the good of John and Emmie."

I nod as I watch him laugh with Steve. He looks over at me and his eyes darken to a forest green as he leans back in the chair, relaxed.

"So what's the plan?" Cara asks.

"I'm going home with him."

"I love that you call it home now. We just want you to be happy. He seems to make you happy."

"He does." Evan winks at me and my insides turn to jelly. *He definitely does.* "I listed the house and I'm going to have some of the stuff in storage shipped to New Hampshire. It feels so strange to have this chapter of my life coming to an end."

"It's not the end, Beth. It's the beginning. And I can't wait to see the next chapter."

"Me, too."

CHAPTER 33

Evan

I have a surprise for you.

"I have a surprise for you," I say as I lay my duffle bag on top of her bag. It was nice to spend a few days with Cara and Steve, but it's time to go home. The inn is busy and we have to get back, but we've already planned another trip out here in the spring.

"What is it? You know I hate surprises." She looks at me and tilts her head, curious.

"You'll like this one," I say confidently.

I feel a warm glow flow through me. Hope. I am looking forward to going home to the inn. *Home.* Beth at the inn feels like home to me. Complete. It feels like everything is in front of us now and it's all good things to look forward to.

Our ride arrives and we hug Cara and Steve. "Thank you for everything."

"You always have a home in Freedom Valley anytime you want to come visit," I tell them.

Beth thinks we're going to the airport to fly home today, but we're not. I have something else planned for us. Cara winks at me and holds the door for us. She and Steve know; they helped me plan it.

We slide into the back of the car that Beth thinks is taking us to the airport and she sinks back into her seat. "I'm going to miss them."

"I can't wait to come back here, and have them out to visit, too."

"Their girls will have a blast at the inn, too. Maybe they can come next year for the fall festival."

"Definitely. It's an annual tradition again." I nod. "Nothing can keep us from doing it now."

Beth is looking out her window and suddenly, she tenses. "Wait, we're not going to the airport." She sits up. "Hey, sir, you missed the turn for the airport."

The driver looks at me for help. I tell her, "Beth, we're not going to the airport."

"Where are we going?"

"I wanted you all to myself for one more day and night

before we go home to the busy inn and everyone else." I pick up her hand in mine and kiss it.

"Aw, well where are we staying?" she asks excitedly. "Is it an inn?"

"Of course it is. We'll call it field research."

Beth laughs. "Okay, let's do this."

We pull up to The Sage Hill Inn and our driver unloads our bags. A gentleman about our age is waiting for us. "Welcome to Sage Hill," he says pleasantly.

I reach for Beth's hand and we walk in together. It's fall in Texas, too, albeit not near as beautiful as New England in the fall. Maybe I'm biased, but nothing can ever compare to New England in autumn.

The property is stunning. Old but unique, rustic but chic. There's two main buildings and several smaller buildings, just like we have at our inn. Wildflowers speckle the sides of the property, making it feel cozy.

A fire pit area is in the center of the property, with Adirondack style chairs fashioned from older wood circling the pit.

We enter the lobby and stop to read some framed newspaper clippings about the history of the inn. *What a great idea.* We learn that The Sage Hill Inn has been restored by a distant family member and is over a hundred years old.

The lady at the front desk welcomes us warmly. "Checking in?" she asks.

I reach in my back pocket and pull out my wallet. "Reservation under Harper," I tell her.

"Welcome Mr. and Mrs. Harper," she says, and Beth squeezes my hand, quietly acknowledging her error. "I see you've booked our Lavender Casita Countryside view suite. Excellent choice."

In fact, neither of us correct her. Instead, Beth says, "Thank you, we're looking forward to our stay."

"It's early. Is it okay that we check in now?" I ask.

"Not to worry, we're ready for you. You have a couples massage booked at two. Lunch begins at eleven, and dinner at five. The pool, hot tub, and outdoor area are open for your enjoyment until midnight."

"Massages..." Beth whispers at me, her eyes light up. "I've never—"

"Me neither. Let's just go with it," I whisper.

"Alright, here is the code to your cottage. Let us know if you need anything, and I hope you enjoy your stay with us." She smiles and slides over a card.

"Thank you," we reply and head out.

As we step outside, Beth beams. "Oh my gosh, Evan. I am so excited for this."

"Right? We can get ideas, relax, and have some time for us to be alone."

"It was so hard being quiet at Cara and Steve's. Do you think they heard us?"

I just give her a look.

Her face reddens but her eyes darken as she leans up to kiss me.

"You can be as loud as you want here. We'll never see these people again. Hopefully," I add with a smirk.

We step into our cottage to find our bags have already been set in the corner.

Our bedroom has a gorgeous view of the countryside and we have our own private back porch with an outdoor fireplace.

"Evan, look at this," Beth exclaims as I step out onto the porch. A bottle of champagne is chilling in a bucket, surrounded by rose petals. "You did this for me?" she asks, her gaze melting into me.

"Of course. I love you, Beth. I'd do anything for you."

"I'm going in the hot tub," she says. I can barely keep it together as she strips down to her bra and panties. My gaze drops from her eyes to her shoulders to her breasts, and suddenly her bra and panties are on the ground, too.

I ache for her touch. I want to stay in this cottage here in Texas and soak her in for a long time, but I know I get her forever now. She's mine, and she's coming home.

She steps into the hot tub. I turn the jets on and strip down as well. I can't join her because of the transplant surgery, but I can soak my feet.

She gasps in delight. "This feels so good." She puts her

arms up on the ledge and leans in to kiss me.

"How would you feel if our guests were lounging in a hot tub naked at our inn?" she asks with a laugh.

Our inn. Yeah, I like the sound of that.

"I don't think I'd want to know." I chuckle.

"Fair enough."

I crack open the champagne and pour her a glass. A couple of bottles of water are on ice there as well so I open one and take a swig.

She takes the glass and sits beside me. Her hands trace my tattoos on my biceps and chest.

"What do these mean?" she asks as her fingers trace them, and my body aches for her touch.

"I just liked them. I got them done when I was in the Marines. It was the cool thing to do, I guess," I say. "I like them, though. To me, they're art."

"I like them, too," she says as she reaches over and pulls me closer. She is the most beautiful woman I've ever seen. *And I get to call her mine.*

She kisses me deeply and I kiss her back until we're both breathless.

Finally, I can't take it anymore, and I pull her up and out of the water and we grab towels as we head into the luxurious tiled shower. I turn the water on and pull her in, wrapping my arms around her and pulling her up, her legs circling me. I kiss her as a sense of urgency takes over and my hands go down her body, pulling her hips in closer to me as I kiss down her neck and groan as I pull her closer.

"Beth..." I say as I reach down and cup her bottom, pulling her even tighter.

"I need you, Evan. Now," she says with equal urgency and pulls herself tighter to me.

I push back and enter her slowly. I pull her closer and tighter until her hands grip my back and she moans. "Evan..."

Warm water pounds down on us and I take her harder and faster.

I feel her body tense up around mine and let go, gripping me tight as she moans deeper.

I let go and meet her with my own orgasm and our bodies vibrate with new life.

This is us. We get our happily ever after. We get to do life together, exactly how I dreamed.

She gasps in delight again. "That was—"

"So good," we say at the same time.

We finish showering and Beth puts on a sundress and sandals while I pull on my jeans and a white t-shirt.

I feel so relaxed and ready for more time with her. I miss the inn, but we need this.

"Ready for your massage, Mrs. Harper?" I tease.

"Ready, Mr. Harper." She grins back.

EPILOGUE

~

"Hey, how's my lady?" Evan murmurs into my ear as he comes in the back door with Bossy and Chip just as I'm hanging up the phone.

"That was Allie," I tell him.

"Oh, good. How's she doing?"

"Well, apparently she's lost her job and is ready to move home." Evan's eyes warm as I use the word home and that isn't lost on me.

He runs his hand over his scruffy chin. "What about Caleb? Can he travel right now?"

I look at him and grin and because I've been thinking too, and I have an idea to share. But before I can speak, he says, "What?"

"So, Logan's in LA and about to head back here for the holidays. I suggested one of us fly out to get Caleb and then

Logan can drive Allie back with their stuff."

"Logan and my sister? Beth, no. What?" He holds up his hands and his face looks concerned.

"What? Logan's a good guy. He'll be happy to help us, I'm sure. He's already out there, and he's coming here anyway to spend the holidays. It just makes sense."

"Are you playing matchmaker with Logan and Allie?" Margie comes into the kitchen from behind me, popping up after obviously listening to our conversation.

"Well, if I was, I learned from the best."

"She's right, Evan. Logan is practically family, and if he's willing to help, take it. You are not flying out. You're still healing and staying here with Beth. The inn is busier than ever, and we need you both here during high season. I'll go get my boy and come back. I am thrilled to have them coming home."

I pull out my phone to reach out to Logan, grinning at both of them.

When he answers, I tell him my plan.

"I was wondering if you're busy the next week before your vacation starts?"

"Not really. What do you need?"

"We need you to help bring Evan's sister and her things back from California this week."

"You want me to drive from California to New Hampshire? Are you nuts?"

"She just lost her job, and they want to get out here as soon as possible. To come home where they have the support of their family."

"Wait, so you want me to ride across the country in a truck with a woman I've never met? Beth, that's insane. What does Evan say about this?"

I look over at Evan brooding over his coffee. "He's... grateful. Margie nixed him from doing it himself since he's still recovering and supposed to be taking it easy."

"What if we hate each other and we're miserable for days? If I do this, you owe me big," he grumbles, sighing heavily.

"She's down in Poway, south of you. Can you be there Saturday? Margie is flying in Saturday and out the following morning with Caleb. I'd come out but... I don't think that's a great idea right now since I'm under intense deadlines with the new book."

"Okay, but you're doing a few interviews," he says.

"Deal."

"Text me her address and phone number. This sounds like a bad idea, Beth. You're lucky you're like a sister to me."

"Thank you, Logan! Evan says thank you too."

"Yeah, yeah. Tell him hi for me. I gotta go into my next meeting. I'll go down to Poway Friday night and get a hotel."

"Love you!"

"Love you, too."

Evan looks at me, his forehead creased with worry. "You

seem pretty happy with your plan."

I just smile at him. "You get Allie and Caleb home safe. I finally get to meet them. And Logan is coming for the holidays. So, yeah, I am happy."

He shakes his head and looks over at the puppies. "I hope this works out."

KEEP UP ON NEW RELEASES

Linktree: linktr.ee/mylevel10life
Newsletter: bit.ly/3Z0QbV2
Shop book merch: www.erinbranscom.com

FOLLOW ME:

Goodreads: www.goodreads.com/mylevel10life
Instagram: @mylevel10life
Facebook: @erinbranscomauthor
Erin's Reading Nook:
www.facebook.com/groups/erinbranscomauthor
Amazon: www.mylevel10life.live
Bookbub: @erinbranscom
TikTok: @mylevel10life

ALSO BY ERIN BRANSCOM

FREEDOM VALLEY SERIES

Falling Inn Love

Baked Inn Love

All Inn Thyme

All Inn Books

Forever Inn Love

Inn the End

NON-FICTION

Writers Inspiring Writers

ABOUT THE AUTHOR

Erin Branscom has read everything she can get her hands on for as long as she can remember. To this day, her favorite place is still the library. In 2021, after a decade of writing novels just for fun, she finally decided to finish a book series and has found writing novels to be her greatest escape. Erin is a passionate author's advocate and loves sharing other authors on Tiktok and Instagram. She lives in Oklahoma and loves traveling and spending time with her husband, four kids, and best friend Molly, a Boston Terrier mix.

ACKNOWLEDGEMENTS

Dusty, Kameron, Ethan, Audrey, and Charlotte, thank you for being the best family I could ever ask for. Thank you for always supporting me on my crazy adventures. I love you all so much!

Mom, thanks for reading my books and encouraging me. Also, thanks for letting me be born. You're the best mom.

Dad and Michael in heaven, I miss you both so much. Every day. It's not fair. I wish you were here. I hope I've made you proud.

Julie and Elizabeth, thanks for being great sisters. We've been through so much in the past few years. Our family is still standing strong.

Auntie Susan and Auntie Paula, you are the best aunt's anyone could ever ask for. I love you both so much.

Molly, you are my best friend in the entire world. Thanks for listening to me talk about all this book stuff and for always keeping me warm in my chair. You deserve all the bones and snuggles.

Erica, you're my favorite human. Period.

Kristi, your taco dates and brainstorming sessions mean the world to me. I'm so thankful for you and your friendship. Also, your success is so inspiring. You work harder than anyone I know!

Willow, thanks for all of the sprints! You're so motivating and inspiring to me!

Brianna, thank you for being my right hand and making everything happen with me.

Enni (Yummy Book Covers), thank you for bringing Freedom Valley to life. I love all these covers so much! Thank you for all that you do! Your books are amazing! You always inspire me.

Brooke Crites (Proofreading by Brooke), thanks for being a great editor.

To everyone reading this… Thank you for taking a chance on me and my Freedom Valley world.

Coming up next in the Freedom Valley Series:
*** All Inn Thyme ***

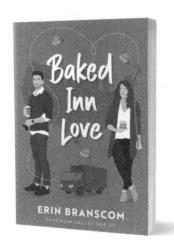

Read the first chapter...

CHAPTER 1

You're fired.

"You're fired."

I'm quiet of the other end, sure I didn't hear correctly.

"I wanted to do this in person, but since you're working from home right now, it has to be done like this."

"What has to be done like this?" I ask my boss Albert as I slide a pan of cookies into the oven.

"We have to let you go. We just can't have people in your... position on the team anymore."

"My position? Meaning what, exactly?" I stand up and walk toward my rickety kitchen table, scored for free from a trash pile on the side of the street, which together with my laptop has been my makeshift office the past several months.

"The position of not being able to give what everyone else on the team is able to give," he says condescendingly.

"And what exactly is everyone else giving right now that I'm not? I work sixty to seventy hours a week and I'm only paid for forty. The only thing I'm not doing is traveling, and almost everyone is working remotely right now. So, what am I not doing?"

I freeze in front of my table, the full reality of what's happening hitting me. I mean, I've always known Albert is a slimeball, but I didn't expect to get fired. I basically lose a piece of my soul every week that I work for him, but I do what I have to do to pay our bills. Caleb is counting on me and only me to provide for him.

"You aren't pulling your weight."

"I see. You know my son just had a major kidney transplant surgery… Firing me means *we* will have no health insurance and no income to pay for medical bills. You're going to cut us off right before the holidays? Do I get a severance package or anything?" I begin to pace my kitchen, my toe rubbing on some of the worn linoleum that is peeling in our trailer that's seen better days.

"Human resources will be getting in touch."

I sit in one of my mismatched chairs and stare at my

computer but can't see a thing through my tears, anger, and fear. I realize I'm checking my work email out of habit while Albert still drones on about how I chose my family over the job he'd graciously handed to me. I realize work emails no longer matter and close the laptop.

I have always tried to keep my personal life separate from work, but I had no choice these past six months with my son being sick. He has a rare childhood kidney disorder and needed a transplant, which he had several weeks ago, and I've been at home with him while he heals since his immune system is still fragile. I've worked day and night at this kitchen table for 393 Creative. Far harder than I should've, apparently.

I never set a timer for my cookies, but I can always smell them right when they're done and know just before they burn. My mom calls it my 'baker's nose.' I've always been a great baker, and that's what I do when I'm stressed. These are pfeffernusse cookies, one of my specialties. The aroma of holiday baking in my kitchen right now is flooded with cinnamon, molasses, cloves, and nutmeg. I wanted to take them back to the hospital for all the nurses we made friends with on the transplant floor where Caleb and Evan had their surgeries. Now, after that phone call, I have bigger things to deal with.

My mom and brother will probably be relieved to hear that I can finally move back home to Freedom Valley. I've stayed in California because, despite how crappy the job was, the insurance was good and covered Caleb's transplant. But now that the transplant is done and there's no job holding me here, I can go back to New Hampshire and help out at the family inn. Evan keeps telling me they will have a job waiting for me whenever I'm ready.

I look over the trailer and mentally try to figure out how to make this work. My thirteen-year-old Toyota Camry has 290k miles on it—I'm not even sure it can make it from our small town of Poway out of California, let alone across the country. I glance over at Caleb, napping on the couch. Even if the car could make it, could his little body handle a cross-country road trip?

I pinch the bridge of my nose and lean back, taking a deep breath. I know what I need to do, but I don't want to do it. I hate asking for help from anyone. Knowing I don't have a choice, I call my brother at the inn. His girlfriend Beth answers. I haven't met her in person yet, but we text and talk on the phone regularly.

"How are you guys doing? Evan stepped out for a minute, but he'll be back soon."

I break down in tears just hearing a friendly voice. It hits me then that I really need to be with my family.

"Allie, are you okay? Is Caleb okay?" Beth's voice is now full of worry.

"We're both okay, but I just lost my job."

"Oh, no. I'm sorry," she says. "What are you going to do?"

"I don't even know. I want to come home."

"Okay, let's make a plan. I'm sure Evan and your mom can help, too," Beth reassures me.

"Right now, I'd love a plan. I need that, badly."

"I think I have an idea. Want to hear it?" she asks.

"Sure, I'll welcome any and all help at the moment," I admit. I'm so tired and overwhelmed from the events of the past few months, I can't even figure out what to make for dinner most nights.

"Okay... I've heard stories about your car, and no offense, but that thing can't make it across the country. What if one of us flies out to get Caleb and brings him here. My friend Logan is leaving LA next week and coming to New Hampshire to spend the holidays with us. He can give you a ride and help you get you and your things back home to the inn."

"What kind of person would volunteer to help a stranger drive across the country?" I have to ask.

"He loves road trips, and besides, he likes to help."

It seems awkward, spending all that time on the road with a person I've never personally met. "I don't know, I don't want to trouble him..."

"He's like family to me, which means he's like family to you now, too. It never hurts to ask."

My parents have always been big on family, and they

raised us in the same way. Even beyond that, we all have a habit of turning friends into family, too. I know how they feel about Beth, and now that I think about it, I'm sure my mom has mentioned Beth's friend Logan to me before. Can I take that chance, though? I realize I've got nothing to lose, and before I can change my mind, I blurt out, "Okay, I guess. I need to start making lists so we can make this happen." I start to cry with relief. "I've wanted to move home for years, Beth. *Years*. I've missed everyone so much."

"Everyone here has missed you, too. We talk about you moving back all the time; everyone is going to be so excited to hear the news. Plus, I can't wait to finally squeeze you both in person! We'll help you and Caleb both get back here quickly and safely."

"Okay, I have to start figuring this out while Caleb is still napping. Thank you, Beth. I appreciate Logan's help. You know, if he's up for it."

"I'm sure he'll do it. Logan loves to drive. And I think we'd all feel better for you to have someone to travel with. I think everyone will worry about you making that trip alone. It will be safer."

I hang up, feeling relieved. When my brother was stationed out here for the Marines, I followed him to go to college here and fell in love with the whole Cali vibe. Surfing, the weather, the food, the fun. But as a single mom, trying to keep us afloat with a job I worked far too many hours at, none of that really applies anymore because I don't get to enjoy the parts of California that I used to enjoy.

For a brief time, there was the hope that Caleb's dad Chris would come around and help us out, but that's never been the case. He refuses to accept Caleb; neither in his life nor as his son. Even Chris's parents want nothing to do with Caleb. You'd think that they'd want to meet their only grandchild, but they have ignored all communication I've tried to have with them. It makes me more sad than angry, because Caleb deserves better.

My family is always there for him, cheering him on, calling him every chance they can, donating their kidneys to literally save his life… The usual. It's been a long time coming for us to finally reunite with them for good; we just have to get home to New Hampshire.

I make a fresh pot of coffee, then put a few warm cookies on a napkin and carry them to my makeshift desk. I open my laptop and check my bank balance. There's a whopping $678 in my checking account. I have one more final paycheck coming, but even factoring that in, my savings won't get us too far.

I need cash, and I need it now. Ever the independent, I refuse to ask Evan or my mom for help. I can do things on my own; I *prefer* to do things on my own.

Looking around at our trailer, I decide that I will sell whatever anyone will buy, assuming anyone wants to buy any of our second- and third-hand furniture and DIY décor. Hopefully that will give me some extra money, and then maybe I will just donate the rest. I don't need to bring too much with me since we have everything at the inn.

Thinking about the drive, I look up how far it is from Poway, California to Freedom Valley, New Hampshire. It's... not close. I calculate gas and food and feel instantly overwhelmed thinking about how I am going to afford this, even if I split everything with Logan.

My eyes drift to my baker's rack and my oven, still warm from the cookies.

I get on the computer and make a post in our neighborhood group offering a pan of homemade organic cinnamon rolls for $40 each. I mention in the post that I'm moving and will be selling everything in the trailer, so I will be happy to make cash deals on anything they can see when people come to pick up their rolls.

Just as I hit the button to post, Caleb stirs on the couch and says, "Mommy."

I head over and snuggle him, telling him the news. "Baby, how would you like to go live with Grandma and Uncle Evan at the inn?"

He smiles big and wraps his little arms around me. "Yes! Do I get to play with his puppies?"

"Yes, buddy, you can play with his puppies. And Kase." Mellie, the housekeeper at The Golden Gable, has a son Kase who is around Caleb's age. "You guys will have so much fun together."

Talking about it out loud and making plans for the move has me starting to feel really excited and less overwhelmed by this new endeavor. Our current neighborhood is a mobile home park, and mostly a retirement community, so there aren't a lot of kids for Caleb to play with. The bonus is that he's had plenty of older, retired grandma and grandpas to spoil him, but I know he'd love to have kids his age to play with now that he's feeling better.

Not to mention, I'm thrilled that Caleb will get to be raised at the inn where my brother and I grew up. That he will get to experience the magic of fall, the smell of Sasha's cooking, and the place my dad loved so much.

Caleb starts playing with his cars while I check my post about the cinnamon rolls. It's only been an hour, but I gasp and put my hand over my mouth when I see I already have forty-three orders. Our community of grandparent-like figures have been so kind to Caleb and me; they've really spoiled us. I'm not surprised they want to support us.

For this number of cinnamon rolls, I'm going to be baking nonstop for the next several days, so I cut it off there. I go through my baking supplies and estimate that I have enough for only a few pans, so I put in a bulk order for more baking supplies to be delivered to me. I hesitate at the cost, but at least this way I can stay home and keep baking.

I realize it's going to be a long night and I pour another cup of coffee. My kitchen becomes a full-on baking zone, stopping only once to make Caleb and me bowls of tomato soup and grilled cheese, which we eat together at the coffee table watching *PJ Masks*.

After a while, Caleb starts yawning so I get him ready for bed, knowing I need to get back to baking anyway.

My phone rings and even though it's late, I know it's Evan.

"Hey, you," I answer on the second ring.

"So, what's going on?" he says, concerned.

"I'm sure Beth filled you in, but it's finally happening, Evan."

"I'm sorry about the job. But, on the bright side, you get to come home now."

"Do you know if she talked to Logan?" I ask hesitantly.

"Yes, that's the other reason I'm calling. He's agreed to help."

"What do you think about that?"

He's quiet for a beat, then finally says, "I'm not against it. Logan's a good guy."

"Why would he say yes to this?" I ask.

"Beth mentioned he usually spends the holidays with her instead of going home to his family, so he was planning on coming here anyway."

"He's really going to drive with me all the way to New Hampshire?"

"That's the plan. Mom's coming to get Caleb. I booked their flights."

"Okay," I say as my oven timer goes off.

"Are you stress-baking again?" he asks.

"Actually, I decided to use up my baking stash to make cinnamon rolls for some of the people in my neighborhood before I go." I don't want to tell him that I need the money, because knowing him, he would just send it to me, and I really don't want him to do that.

"I can't wait to have your cinnamon rolls again. Sasha is tired of baking and could definitely use your help when you get here."

I smile because I know he sees right through my bullshit and still decides not to call me on it.

"Love you, Evan. I gotta get to bed. You probably do, too."

"Love you, too. Can't wait to have you guys home."

We hang up and I look at the clock. Of course there's no bedtime in sight for me right now. I hate lying to Evan, but I need to get to baking if we're going to get out of here.

I catch up on our laundry and make bags for donation in between cinnamon roll orders. I haul the donation piles out to my trunk and wrap the cinnamon rolls once they're cooled and frosted. I add my signature ribbons to each package, including a handwritten thank you card expressing my gratitude for everything our community has done for us.

I finally turn off the oven and fall into bed around four. I know Caleb will probably have me up around seven and I'll need to get started baking again. *I can do this*, I lie to myself as I drift off to sleep.

Keep reading: books2read.com/FVS2

Made in the USA
Las Vegas, NV
27 July 2024